RESE

D1135413

A Star Original

'Hello, Dolly,' said the young man. 'To coin a phrase.'

She said nothing.

'Surprised?'

No words would come. She stared at him.

'Sorry to bring about the reunion in public. But this seemed the only place where I could catch up with you.'

'How did you find me?' she asked at last, speaking as if in pain.

'It took some doing.'

They stood face to face, the bar top between them. 'Half of real ale,' she said, and moved to get it.

'Dolly,' he said pleadingly.

'Go away,' she whispered. 'Go away. Leave me alone.'

He shook his head. 'Never again, Dolly. Not now I've found you again.'

Tears were sparkling at the rims of her eyes. 'Richard,' she said, carefully placing the half-pint before him, 'for pity's sake, drink this and go.'

Also by Lee Mackenzie in *Star*

EMMERDALE FARM   BOOK 10

SHADOWS
FROM THE PAST

Lee Mackenzie

Based on the successful
Yorkshire Television series
originated by Kevin Laffan

A STAR BOOK
published by
the Paperback Division of
W. H. ALLEN & Co. Ltd

A Star Book
Published in 1980
by the Paperback Division of
W. H. Allen & Co. Ltd
A Howard and Wyndham Company
44 Hill Street, London W1X 8LB

Printed in Great Britain by
Richard Clay (The Chaucer Press), Ltd,
Bungay, Suffolk

ISBN 0352 30451 0

CHAPTER ONE

The darkness of an early winter evening lay over the village. Overhead, the stars glinted in a frosty sky. The inhabitants of Beckindale were, most of them, snugly indoors by their firesides, with the curtains drawn against the chill draughts that sneaked in round the old window-frames. Little gleams of light showed from cottages. Old Mrs Farmer was calling home her recalcitrant cat: 'Tibby, Tibby, Tibby!'

The only other sound was the footsteps of a couple pacing the High Street. Matt Skilbeck and Dolly Acaster were making their way to the church.

'Come on now, Matt, you can do it,' Dolly coaxed in a low voice.

'I knew it a minute ago,' Matt muttered. He drew his brows together and began again: '*Crysts cross me spede, and Saint Nycholas! Therof had I nede ...*' He paused. '*Had I nede ... Had I nede ...*'

'*Therof had I nede; it is wors than it was,*' prompted Dolly, who had the book of the medieval Nativity Play in her hands. 'It's difficult, isn't it, Matt? I wonder what it means?'

'By the time t'vicar's got us word-perfect, happen we'll know,' Matt said with a faint grin. 'I think *he* knows, all right.'

'I think he's ever so clever,' Dolly said.

'Well, of course –'

'No, I mean, cleverer than most vicars. Cleverer than David, for instance.'

It was a bit of a surprise to Matt to hear her say that. In general, he had the impression that Dolly felt no one could be better at the business of being a vicar than David Hockley – not that being a vicar was a business, exactly. It was a career, a calling.

5

And luckily for Matt, David had been 'called' by his bishop to take over the care of an inner city parish where his abilities could be used to the full among the young people. It wasn't in Matt's nature to be jealous, but he had experienced a great sense of relief at David's going. David was young, handsome, very outgoing and lovable. It had seemed to Matt only natural that Dolly should be fond of him.

Inevitable, too – for Dolly had been living in the vicarage with David. Viewed in practical terms, this had been a very sensible arrangement. Amos Brearley didn't want her living-in at the Woolpack where she worked, there was nowhere else where she could find digs, and David had needed someone to dust and tidy up for him. Just as Matt couldn't experience jealousy, David couldn't feel uneasiness about his reputation. It didn't bother him in the least that the elders of the parish were scandalised by this set-up.

No one would ever know whether perhaps the Bishop had been more attuned to the ordinary man in the street's opinion. His Lordship was no stuffed shirt, but neither was he a fool. Perhaps his decision to move David Hockley had something to do with the situation with regard to his 'lodger'. Whatever the reason, the Rev. Mr Hockley had been gone from Beckindale some three months now, too busy with his new parish to think of coming back for a visit.

Matt knew that Dolly wrote to him, and received letters in reply. But a man fifty miles away isn't nearly so formidable as when he's hurrying around the neighbourhood, looking friendly and good-natured. The only drawback was that Dolly didn't get on so well with the new vicar.

The Rev. Mr Hinton was a man of quite a different kind. He was older than David, a bit thick round the middle and by no means so quick to smile nor so modern in his outlook. At first he made no comment about Dolly's occupation of one of the upstairs rooms. He allowed the arrangement to go on as before. But when she tidied his books, he untidied them again almost at once. When she cooked him a nice piece of fish for his lunch, he said regretfully that he wasn't ready to eat yet. When she got his evening meal ready a little early

6

in view of the fact that he'd had no lunch, he confessed that he'd had a real Italian lasagne at a restaurant in Hotten just over an hour ago.

In a word, he was a man who liked to eat when he felt like eating, not at set times. He didn't want his books tidied up for him. He didn't want to be talked to when he didn't feel like talking. He was more reticent than David, more interested perhaps in things of the spirit than in social welfare. He spent long periods in meditation; he worked very hard over his sermons.

The long and short of it was, Dolly became aware that she was a nuisance. Mr Hinton would never have said so – wild horses wouldn't have dragged the word out of him. But, directly challenged, he had to admit that he was used to living on his own.

'You see, Miss Acaster,' he murmured, lifting heavy dark eyebrows in apology, 'I've been a widower for some time now, and I've come to terms with solitude. To tell the truth, I enjoy it. Solitude and loneliness aren't the same thing, you know – to be alone with yourself and God is the best company in the world.'

'So I'm putting you out by staying on here,' Dolly said with a rueful smile. 'I've had a feeling I wasn't "Top of the Pops" in your estimation, vicar.'

'Oh, please – Miss Acaster –'

'It's quite all right. I should have realised it wouldn't work. I'll see if I can find a place to move to, Mr Hinton. But it may take a while.'

'No hurry, no hurry.' Poor Mr Hinton ... Dolly understood that he felt unchristian over the whole thing, but she sympathised with his need to have the place to himself. It's not everybody that likes or needs company.

She knew only too well how difficult it was to find digs in Beckindale. She'd been through it all before. If only Amos would be more welcoming to her! But, like Mr Hinton, Amos was set in his ways. 'I can't be doing with female persons in the living quarters of the Woolpack,' he'd told his partner. And no amount of persuasion from Henry Wilks was going to change him.

Dolly had been through the usual routine of looking in the *Hotten Courier*'s small ads, perusing noticeboards outside the tobacconist and newsagent in Hotten and Connelton, asking around among friends. Weeks had gone by. Mr Hinton had made no complaint, but she had felt more and more of an encumbrance.

From this difficult situation she'd been rescued by Joe Sugden. 'Look here, Dolly,' he'd said to her one evening over a pint at the bar, 'strikes me I'm being a right dog-in-the-manger! I can solve your problem for you in a minute.'

'You can? How's that?'

'Why don't you move into Demdyke?'

Joe had a cottage in Demdyke Row in Beckindale, bought over a year before when he was hoping to get wed to Kathy Gimbel. That hope had turned to dust and ashes; Kathy had left him, and the cottage was his intermittent home these days when he wasn't at Emmerdale. Annie Sugden would have preferred him to move back to the farm permanently, but never said so. Now, as he listened to Dolly wondering where she could try next, it occurred to him that it was time to take that decision.

Dolly misunderstood. 'Oh ... er ... I don't know, Joe. Folks were a bit funny about me and David. I don't know how they'd react if I moved in with you ...'

Joe grinned and gave her a playful pat on the hand wielding a cleaning cloth over the bar's surface. 'Chance would be a fine thing,' he teased. 'Nay, lass, you can have t'place to yourself. I'm moving out.'

'Really?' She looked delighted, then her lively features showed doubt. 'You doing it just so's to give me a place to live?'

'No, I've had it in my mind. Ma'd like me to be at home, and it makes sense to be right on the spot at the farm.' He frowned at her in pretended menace. 'Mind, you'd have to pay a very high rent – and regular. Otherwise, it's out on your ear!'

'It's ever so kind of you, Joe. Wouldn't you rather sell it?'

'Well ... I would, I suppose.' It was dishonest to pretend otherwise. 'But it'll always fetch a good price. There's no hurry to put it on t'market.'

Dolly had been more grateful than she could say. She intended to move her belongings to Demdyke this very evening, after she'd taken part in the rehearsal of the Nativity Play.

'Sure you don't want me to give you a hand?' Matt inquired, glad to let the learning of his lines go by the board for a moment.

'Nay, I'm only taking a few bits this evening,' Dolly replied. 'Besides, you ought to stay and get on with the rehearsal. You're one of the stars, after all! Me, I'm just a dogsbody.'

Matt laughed. 'Atween you and Ma, I'll be decked out like a sheikh! Are you sure shepherds in Galilee wore such bright colours?'

'It's got to have a bit of richness, Matt. It's competing with all the old beams and panelling, and the stained glass windows. And the Virgin Mary has to be in dark blue. So really the only way to put colour into the costumes is to have the Wise Men and the shepherds in reds and ambers and greens.'

Dolly had a gift for stage design. Last year she'd decorated the shabby old village hall for a community concert, and though she'd upped and left before the event, everyone had said how beautiful the place looked as a result of her work. She and Annie Sugden were responsible for the costumes for the present venture; Dolly had designed them, Annie was making them. Almost everyone in Beckindale had been roped in: Sam Pearson was making a 'lamb' for Matt to carry to the Manger, Henry Wilks was in charge of the lighting, the constable for the district was producing metal boxes and containers for the Gifts of the Wise Men, the village bellringers were practising a special peal for the end of the play, and all the mothers of small angelic-looking children were winding silver or gold paper round hoops to make haloes for the Heavenly Choir.

'Come on now, Matt – once more,' Dolly coaxed. '*Crysts cross me spede, and Saint Nycholas ...*'

'I need more than Saint Nycholas to speed me,' sighed Matt.

9

'I just can't seem to remember what order the words come in.'

'It's because it's all in this old-fashioned English. Funny, isn't it – to think that folks around here performed this same play about five hundred years ago –'

'And sounded quite different! Can't understand why they didn't speak proper English.'

'But that's because ...' Dolly broke off and peered up at him, just in time to track the hint of a smile on his deadpan face – and knew he was pulling her leg. 'Oh, you!' she scolded. 'Anything not to have to memorise your lines. Come along now, Matt. *Crysts cross me spede ...*'

Dutifully he took up the lines, and they paced on towards the parish church where the rehearsal was to take place. Joe Sugden, driving through Beckindale on his way to keep a date, gave them a cheerful toot on his horn as he caught them in his headlights.

As he drove on to keep his date with Lesley, he thought: 'They make a good pair. I wonder if anything will ever come of it?'

At home, he knew, feelings on that score were somewhat divided. His mother was in favour of Matt remarrying; even though it meant putting Peggy into the past, Ma wanted Matt to be happy again. Life had been hard on him, and Ma grieved for her son-in-law. If Dolly could give him again what he'd had with her daughter Peggy, Annie Sugden would be only too delighted to start on wedding plans.

Grandad was more difficult to fathom, Joe thought. He was against any kind of change, and if Matt were to settle down with Dolly that would mean a change. Yet even there, things were different. Grandad had been twice to Rome in the past year. By air, too. The first time, it had been achieved by a subterfuge; old Sam had had a little setback and the doctor had put it forward that he oughtn't to spend all the winter in the cold of the dales. Henry Wilks had rung Brother Jack in Rome, asking him to beg the old man to take the trip on the pretext that Jack needed his help with background for a book. Naturally, as soon as he knew he was needed, Sam had

10

been packed and ready to go.

But, stranger yet, Jack actually had got the idea for a book from his grandfather. He'd asked him back a few months later to go on with the research. The book's provisional title was *One Man In His Time*, and was actually about Sam Pearson – though how anybody could find anything worth writing about in Sam's life, his grandson Joe couldn't imagine.

There was no doubt that it had changed Grandad. Why, in times gone by he'd have retreated from an aeroplane as if it was the Horseman of the Apocalypse. Yet now, he even got up to take a call from Rome with total sang-froid, and would chat on to Jack as if it was run of the mill. So happen if Matt actually ever persuaded himself that Dolly liked him as more than just a friend, Grandad might take it quite well. But whenever it was hinted at, he frowned and muttered and huffed and puffed. That might just be habit, though, Joe said to himself with a grin.

Lesley Gibson had walked down to the crossroads to be collected for their date. She waved as he drew alongside – a tall girl in a loose leather blouson, tight trousers, and high-heeled boots.

'Hello there,' she called. 'Bang on time – that's what I like in a man.'

'I'm not saying what it is I like in a girl,' Joe rejoined, opening the car door to let her clamber in.

'You don't need to. I know you're atracted to me because I'm a daughter of the best brewing family in the district,' she laughed.

'Oh, 'twas not her beauty alone that won me,' carolled Joe, 'Oh no, 'twas the beer in the vats ever brewing, That made me love Lesley, the hops of Tralee.'

'Gerron wi' thee,' she said easily as she snuggled up against him. 'Where we going?'

'Dunno. Where'd you fancy?'

'What I'd like is a nice warming rum and coke.'

'You can get that anywhere.'

'Ah, but only Miller's Arms at Robblesfield keeps real, specially imported Jamaica rum.'

11

'The worst of taking out a girl from a brewing family,' Joe complained to no one in particular, 'is she knews more about pubs than you do.'

They were pleased with each other, but each knew it would never go very deep. Joe was still smarting over the break-up of his relationship with Kathy Gimbel, and Lesley had made it understood from the outset that she wasn't ready to settle down with any one man. A bit of a woman's-libber, was Lesley. Well, that suited Joe. He needed companionship and gaiety; Lesley was ready to offer those blessings without expecting too much in return.

The Miller's Arms in Robblesfield was a very old pub, as old as the Beckindale Woolpack, if not older. Moreover, it was a bit more welcoming. Henry Wilks did his best to make the Woolpack warm and friendly but Amos always insisted the clientele liked it just the way it was – worn, spare, and very much a man's pub. The Miller's Arms hadn't allowed itself to be tarted up in any way, but it had more comfortable chairs, warmer lighting, and a roaring fire in an old-fashioned fireplace.

'How do,' said Fred Teaker as they came in. 'Sugden, isn't it? Fra Beckindale.'

'That's right. On enemy territory, ain't we!'

'Not while cricket's off,' Fred said with a rather sour smile. 'Friendly enemies, that's what we are, eh?'

'Right you are. We'll have two rum and cokes.'

'Aye.' Fred measured the rum. 'Can't get this in t'Woolpack, can you! How's Mr Brearley?'

'As well as can be expected.'

'You what? He's been ill?'

'Nay. He's as well as can be expected of Amos.'

Fred Teaker actually smiled. 'Know what you mean,' he said, and with a nod left them.

'Enemies?' Lesley said as she followed Joe to a quiet table. 'In what way?'

'Oh, it's all this cricket rubbish. We play a match every year against Robblesfield. A right good team they've got, too. They've a bowler as'd make Lever look poorly. You should see us in t'season – snooping on each other to find out what tactics we're going to use.'

'Sounds serious!'

'It is, wi' some of the folks around here. More important than the Test. My grandad's one of the worst. You should have seen him last summer, trying to work out how to get the upper hand so as to keep the Butterworth Ball.'

'And what, may one ask, is the Butterworth Ball?'

'We-ell ... It's a ball.'

'You don't say.'

'Haven't you ever seen it? In the niche behind the bar at t'Woolpack.'

'Can't say I have. A trophy, you mean? Siver or gold?'

'Nay, it's just a ball.'

Lesley raised her arched eyebrows at him. 'You mean, an ordinary cricket ball.'

'Well ... yes.'

'And you compete for it?'

'Yes.'

'And whoever wins the match gets to keep it in a niche?'

'Yes.' Joe began to laugh. 'Sounds daft! But tempers rise and hearts get broken over it every year.'

'Who says,' Lesley wondered, 'that Yorkshiremen are phlegmatic?'

'Well, I don't, for one. I don't even know what it means.'

Pleased with each other, they had an enjoyable evening. Around ten they left the Miller's Arms and headed for Beckindale, but with no intention of saying goodnight just yet. Joe invited Lesley for a cup of tea at Demdyke Row; she accepted his invitation.

So when Dolly walked in with a small suitcase containing her cosmetics and shampoos, it was to find them deep in the sofa and a rather torrid embrace.

'Oh,' she said, embarrassed.

Lesley sat up. 'Hello,' she said, not the least put out. 'It's Dolly, isn't it? Don't just stand there – come in. We were just having a little get together.'

'I ... er ... I didn't mean to butt in –'

13

'Come in, come in,' Joe said, pink with confusion but trying not to stammer. 'It's your house now.'

'Nay, I ... you ...'

'We were just leaving.'

'Oh, Joe,' laughed Lesley. 'We'd only just got here.'

'Come on.'

'But isn't this your home?'

'Not while Dolly's here –'

'I'll only be a minute,' Dolly said in utter misery.

'Nonsense, take your time. Come on, Lesley.'

'Where are we going?' Lesley asked.

'How the dickens do I know?' Joe replied, dragging her out.

Dismayed, Dolly stood back to let them pass. As she went by, Lesley flashed her a smile. 'The cave-man touch,' she said. And then, not intending to let it reach Dolly as they went out into the night, 'All the same, it's a bit much, not having a place to call your own.'

The following morning Matt dropped by at the Woolpack to ask Dolly hear him repeat the next page of the text of the Nativity play. Sensitive as he was to all her moods, he knew at once she was upset. When he got back to the farm for the midday meal, his mother-in-law happened to be on her own in the kitchen. She was just putting the receiver back on the telephone.

'There,' she said with some satisfaction, 'I've got that sorted.

'What's that?'

'I've arranged with Tippy Srawbrook to have the Scout troop tidy up the garden for t'vicar. It's not fair, you know, letting him move in to a place that needs so much done to it. That garden's a wilderness.'

'Reckon it is,' he agreed.

'You're a bit early for dinner. It's oxtail.'

'That's nice.'

She glanced at him sharply as she picked up the oven gloves. He was abstractedly turning a knife round on its haft, his thoughts miles away. He came to himself with a start when the knife hit the fork set out in its place for the forthcoming meal.

'Something wrong?' Annie inquired, busying herself with the oven door.

He shook his head.

'Saw Dolly, did you? What did she think of your learning of your lines?'

'I can't seem to keep 'em in my head.' He hesitated. 'Dolly was a bit upset.'

'About what?'

'This arrangement she's got with Joe to use Demdyke.'

'Oh?' said his mother-in-law. She got the casserole of ox-tail out of the oven and set it on a fireproof stand on the draining board. 'I thought that was a good idea? Joe isn't there much.'

'No, but when he is ...' He broke off. He had no intention of discussing Joe's private affairs. 'Thing is, Ma, he told Dolly he was going to sort of come in and out now and again.'

'Well, that's all right, isn't it?'

'But you know ... that's what's wrong at t'vicarage. She's there when Mr Hinton don't want her, and not there when it would be a blessing to her to have the place to herself.'

'But surely with Joe ...?'

'It's no use, they'll get to feeling awkward with each other, just as it has with t'vicar.'

Annie had taken the lid off the casserole. A cloud of fragrant steam rose towards her. She dipped a spoon into the contents, tasted it, nodded to herself, and brought it to the table. As she went back to fetch the vegetables she remarked, 'You like Dolly, don't you, Matt?'

He was surprised. 'Of course.'

'You feel involved in seeing her nicely settled.'

'Aye ... Only in a friendly way, you know. I'm not saying it's more.'

'I understand that.' She went to the door to open it and call, 'Dinner's ready, Dad.'

From somewhere a long way off, her father's voice replied. 'Coming ...'

'He's still working on that blessed lamb of yours,' she said

15

with a smile as she came back to set plates by the casserole dish. She sat down and began to serve the food. 'How would you feel if she lived here, Matt?'

'Who?'

'Dolly, of course.'

'Here?' He was too startled to take it in all at once. His open, gentle face was creased in frowns.

'I'd quite like another woman around the place. It's a bit much now and again, tha knows, being the only woman in a houseful of men!' They both smiled, and she resumed, 'To be honest, I'd quite appreciate a bit of help about the place. Seems to me Dolly would be just the right lass.'

But Matt knew the hazards. 'How about Grandad?'

'He likes Dolly well enough.'

'But living-in here? He'd happen not take to that so easy.'

'You can leave that to me,' she said with confidence. 'How'd you yourself feel?'

Matt took his time before answering. There were many aspects to his mother-in-law's idea. First there was the change it would mean in the household itself. Say what she might, Annie wouldn't persuade her father without a struggle. And Sam had a way of making his disapproval felt. Then there was what it might mean to Dolly herself. Dolly never seemed to have the chance to make a home for herself; she was being bandied about like a package. How would she feel about settling in with another new lot of landlords?

Lastly, there were his own feelings. Matt knew that Dolly liked him, but whether it went any deeper than that he couldn't tell. It didn't seem probable; he felt he wasn't the kind of chap to make a big impact on a girl like Dolly. At the moment, he felt he could draw back from his friendship with her and never feel the worse for it. But if she came to live at Emmerdale, happen she'd wind herself into his heart to such an extent that he wouldn't recover if she then went away from Beckindale.

But it was selfish to think about himself. Dolly needed a place to stay and here was Annie offering one. 'I reckon it might solve a lot of problems if she came here,' he said. 'As long as you're not doing it just for me?'

16

She gave a little laugh and passed him a plate of steaming food. 'I would do it just for you, Matt,' she confessed. 'But I'd be helping myself, too. So, shall I ask her – or will you?'

Matt coloured at the thought of having to offer the invitation. It would be like putting Dolly under an obligation to him. 'I'd rather you,' he said.

'Well I will, then.'

They could hear Sam's footsteps on the yard outside. Matt said quickly, 'Happen you're doing it to help yourself, Ma – but thanks!'

When Annie made the offer to Dolly, the leap of relief and thankfulness in her eyes spoke for her without the need of words. 'Oh, Mrs Sugden!' she breathed.

'Would you like to?'

'Would I!'

'Don't forget, I'd expect a bit of housework and so on. It's not just a one-sided affair.'

'Of course not. I'd be delighted to lend a hand. You know that. Only ... I wonder if you really ...'

'It's a bit much being on my own with men all the time,' Annie assured her. 'It's all football and cricket and politics. They never discuss fashions or cake recipes or ... or ...'

'Babies, and weddings ...'

'Or W.I. programmes, or the cost of coffee and sugar ...'

'Or anything really important,' Dolly ended with a giggle. 'Oh, I do sympathise with you! It'll be lovely being with a family. Living on your own's no fun.'

'Then there's no reason why it can't be a happy arrangement all round. And that will leave Joe free to use Demdyke whenever he feels like it.'

Dolly eyed Annie, wondering how much Matt had told her about the incident last night. Very little, she guessed. Matt wasn't the sort to pass on gossip. But she felt sure Annie could put two and two together without help from anyone.

'When would you like me to move in?'

'Soon's you like, my dear.'

'Would tonight be too early?'

'My word,' Annie said, nodding in appreciation, 'you really

mean it when you say you want to come.'

'Oh, I do, I can't tell you!' Dolly blurted. 'I'm that fed up of being a sort of square peg in other people's round holes!'

This conversation had taken place at the Woolpack just after the midday closing time. Amos was all agog to hear what Annie had wanted to say to Miss Acaster, for whom she had asked specially. When Dolly told him she was moving into the farm, he didn't know whether to be pleased or miffed.

'Not very convenient, is it?' he remarked. 'It's a long way from Emmerdale to t'Woolpack.'

'A long way? It's only fifteen minutes walk, and no time at all on my scooter.'

'Hm,' said Amos. 'I'd be obliged if you wouldn't park that machine so that I can't get my bike out, Miss Acaster. If I'm called out by the *Hotten Courier* on an important story, it would be most awkward trying to get it out from behind that thing.'

'I'm sorry. I thought it would be best to put it in back alley rather than take up customers' parking space, Mr Brearley.'

'Well, see it doesn't happen again.' He let a moment go by. 'So you're moving in at Emmerdale, then.'

'Yes, this evening.'

'After we close, I hope, Miss Acaster.'

'Of course – in my own time.'

'And all this decorating you're going to do for Christmas – that'll be in your own time an' all, I hope?'

She was taken aback. 'I ... er ... I only just thought ... I haven't actually planned anything ...'

As if on cue, Henry Wilks came in carrying a Christmas tree. 'There,' he said with satisfaction. 'What d'you think of that?'

The question was addressed to both of them. Dolly clapped her hands and said: 'Doesn't that look good?' Amos glared and said: 'Don't put it down there!'

Henry paid no heed. He set the tree down in its tub in a spot between the door and the fireplace.

'Did you hear me, Mr Wilks?'

'It's got to go there, Amos. Where else would you put it?'

'You know very well I don't want one at all! Trees are better out than in!'

'But you've got to have a Christmas tree, Mr Brearley,' Dolly protested.

'I don't see the necessity. They only get knocked over, and if you put lights on 'em they fuse, and they shed needles all over everything.'

'You can spray it with stuff –'

'Spray what?'

'The tree. To prevent the needles falling off.'

'Can you?' Henry said, amazed. 'My word, Dolly, you're a knowledgeable lass!'

'It's all expense,' Amos objected. 'First a tree, and then a tub to put it in, and then stuff to spray it with –'

'And then ornaments to trim it with,' Henry continued. 'Is there no end to this outpouring of money?'

'You may laugh, Mr Wilks, but mark my word, someone'll knock it over, and we'll have them little bits of curvy glass all over everything and somebody'll put his hand on a bit and get hurt, and they'll *sue* us –'

'And a Merry Christmas to you, Amos!'

'And that's another thing! It's ages till Christmas – that tree'll be past it by Christmas Day.'

'I shall know how it feels,' Henry said with a sigh. 'Dolly, what was that you were saying yesterday about making a wreath of holly and evergreens?'

'A wreath?' cried Amos. 'Who's dead, then?'

'Not that kind of wreath, Mr Brearley,' Dolly explained. 'It's what the Germans call a *Winterkranz* –'

'I'm not having them foreign ideas here! Bad enough when folk ask for funny lager with funny names! And another thing, Miss Acaster! If you're planning to see anything of that young man between now and Christmas, you'll have to cut down on the time you spend helping with that Nativity Play.'

Dolly stared at him.

'What young man?'

'The young man who was in here at lunch time. Don't think

19

I didn't see the way he was eyeing you.'

'Now, now, Amos,' Henry soothed. 'It's natural that young men should eye Dolly. She's a very attractive young lady.'

Dolly flashed him a mischievous smile. 'Thank you, kind sir. Does that mean I can ask for an increase in salary, because I attract customers?'

'Miss Acaster!' Amos was shocked. He pulled down the fronts of his waistcoat with dignity. 'No one can say that I use any temptations of that kind to get men into my bar.'

'But you admit it attracted a young man in at lunch time today,' Henry put in.

'I don't know so much. He came in and took up a spot behind that group of Ministry men who are doing an advisory survey for Harbottle's. Seemed to me more like he wanted to keep out of her way, not catch her eye.'

'Get on with you,' Henry said, too busy with his tree to pay much heed.

But Dolly seemed struck. She finished stacking clean glasses then turned to Amos. 'What was he like then, this fellow?'

'What d'you mean, what was he like? What difference does it make? A customer's a customer –'

'But you just said, if I was going to spend much time with him, I'd have to give up the Nativity Play. You must have thought he was a likely prospect.'

'That's no way to talk. I was just saying ... He did seem a bit keen so I thought ... Didn't he speak to you after all?'

She shook her head.

'Funny. He asked where you lived.'

'What?' A momentary alarm glinted in her eyes. 'Did you tell him?'

'Of course not,' Amos said, affronted. 'I don't hold with that kind of thing – assignations in a bar! I told him he must ask you himself.'

Henry turned. 'But he didn't?' he asked, looking at Dolly. He had heard the faint alarm in her voice when she questioned Amos.

'No,' she said. 'No, he didn't.'

Henry rose from his stooping position by the tree and

came close to her. Having a daughter of his own, he could understand how girls could sometimes feel vulnerable and a bit scared. 'It's all right,' he reassured her. 'Too shy to speak, it seems. He's not the troublesome kind.'

'No,' she agreed. She looked at him in gratitude, not only for the words but for the instinct of kindness that had brought him to her side. 'No, he's just a passing stranger, I expect.'

The man who had spoken to Amos Brearley was indeed a stranger in Beckindale. But, judging by the attention he was giving the village, he didn't intend to be a stranger for long. That afternoon he drove back and forth four times through the village, and on his fourth trip witnessed Dolly, almost unrecognisable in her scooter helmet and puttering along at a good speed, heading out over the bridge. He watched her disappear over the first little incline.

Then, with a strange expression that was half a smile and half a frown, he put his car in gear and followed her.

CHAPTER TWO

Late that same night, Matt was walking home. He'd had a long session in Mr Hinton's living-room with the vicar and the other 'Shepherds' to try to help them with not only the memorising but the understanding of their lines. Afterwards one of the participants, Ted Barker, a widower, had invited the men to his house for bottled beer and chat. Since Ted was an influential local builder, the talk had ranged over the prospects for Beckindale and the area surrounding.

Afterwards, to clear his head and because he loved the quiet of the night-time countryside, Matt had taken the long way round the village to come to the bridge. He was passing the Woolpack, dark and with everyone apparently asleep, when he glimpsed a shadowy figure slip from the back alley and

21

away from him, up the main street and towards the church where the path led nowhere except on towards the vicarage and the open fields.

Matt paused. He was on the verge of shouting, 'Hi there – what's to do?' But then he thought, suppose it's some naughty youngster slinking home from a night on the tiles. Suppose it's a husband who's had a bit too much and slept it off in a barn before heading for bed. Suppose ... well, there could be any of a hundred innocent reasons. Without giving it any more thought, and conscious of the fact that it was getting on for one am and he had to be at work in about four and a half hours, he hurried on.

Thus he missed the great drama of a few seconds later. The lights came on at the back of the Woolpack. The hand that switched them on was that of mine host. Amos Brearley came staggering downstairs, pulling on his dressing-gown.

'Who's there?' he called. 'Anybody there?'

He'd put on the light over the landing and the stairs. He now lit up the back room of the pub, where he mostly lived and had his being. It was from somewhere in this area that the sound had come.

He stood to one side of the doorway. 'Come out!' he called. 'I've got you covered.' With what, he didn't specify. The weapon he was holding was in fact the poker from the old-fashioned fireside-set by the empty fireplace in his bedroom.

No response. Dead silence. After a long moment, Amos took a peek. There was no one in the back room. Nothing stirred, except a drip from the tap into the sink.

He walked in. The poker was well to the fore. 'Come out,' he commanded. He looked behind the armchair and behind the fridge, but no one was skulking there.

A sound behind him made him whirl. He brandished the poker.

'Hey-up, Amos!' cried Henry Wilks, leaping back. 'It's me!'

'Oh, Mr *Wilks* ...' Amos leaned against the fridge until his heart had stopped going pit-a-pat. 'What a fright you gave me.'

'I gave you? How do you think I felt, having a poker shaken in my face?' Henry came into the room, tying the cord of his silk dressing-gown. 'Sheffield steel, is that,' he re-marked, eyeing the weapon. 'It could have split my skull.'

'You shouldn't have crept up on me –'

'I didn't creep. I just came downstairs in the normal way.' Henry smoothed back the fringe of hair round the sides of his bald head. 'What on earth are you doing down here in t'middle of t'night?'

'I'm catching a burglar, that's what,' Amos said, very fierce and confident. He felt better now Mr Wilks was here. But to do him justice, he'd been prepared to take on whoever he found downstairs.

'What burglar?' Henry asked. He looked about. There was no one in the room except themselves.

'There was somebody here. I heard him.'

'Heard what?'

'I heard a . . . There was a . . . A sound.'

'You probably woke yourself with your own snoring, Amos.'

'I do not snore, Mr Wilks,' said his partner, offended.

'How do you know you don't? Have you ever stayed awake to listen?'

'How could I stay awake and . . .' Amos realised his leg was being pulled. 'This is serious, Mr Wilks. Someone is in the Woolpack.'

'Rubbish.'

'I tell you, I heard a sort of a thud –'

'A sickening thud?'

'Eh?' Amos read very little and knew nothing about well-worn cliches from the thrillers of bygone years. 'It was more of a . . . chunk.'

'A chunk of what?'

'A sound like a chunk. Like this.' Amos picked up a jug from the top of the fridge and put it down on the metal top. 'Like that, only louder.'

'It was something falling over.'

'What, then?' Amos waved a hand. 'Nothing's fallen over.'

'Aye,' Henry said, rather dry. 'Everythings just as usual.'

'In here,' Amos agreed. 'But who knows where else he's been?' He suddenly clutched his dressing-gown in the region

23

of his heart. 'The till!' he cried.

He rushed out and into the bar. Henry followed, much more slowly. Accustomed as he was to Amos's funny ways, this amused him only a little. As a man approaches the golden years, he needs his sleep.

Amos went to the till, rang up 'no sale', and found the money still there. It's to be understood that this money wasn't the whole day's takings. Those were upstairs under lock and key in a box below Amos's bed. The money in the till was a peace-offering to any burglar who might get in: Amos reasoned that if a man got something, he wouldn't creep upstairs and murder you in your bed.

He had a low opinion of how much a burglar would be satisfied with. Nevertheless the one pound note, one fifty pence piece, and four twopence pieces were still there.

'You see?' Henry said. 'Nobody's got in. If they had, they'd have taken that.'

Amos was shaken. Then he said, 'I disturbed him at it. That's what it is! The chunk I heard – that was the till being pushed shut.'

'Funny sort of burglar who bothers to close the till when he's disturbed,' Henry rejoined, rubbing the back of his neck and stifling a yawn. 'Come on, Amos, let's get back to bed.'

'Nay, Mr Wilks, I tell thee – someone's been in here. I can feel it.'

'Clairvoyant, are you?'

'Mr Wilks, I'm C of E as well you know,' Amos said. He was examining the contents of the saloon bar – in his opinion the prints on the wall and the copper cans holding rather dusty arrangements of dried flowers were valuable. But they were all there.

'Anything missing?' Henry inquired, following him on his inspection.

'No, not that I can see . . .'

But he was looking worried. Henry looked at him and realised that though it was all a false alarm, for Amos the worry was genuine. He put a friendly hand on his shoulder for a moment. 'Come on, lad, we've work to do in the morning.

Let's get back to bed.'

Amos was forced to the conclusion that he'd had a dream. But to reassure himself of his safety when he returned to dreamland, he went to check the front door.

It swung open in his hands.

'Mr Wilks,' he breathed.

Henry came to his side. For a moment he was taken aback. 'Well!' he muttered.

'There you are!' Amos cried. 'That's how he got out! That's why he'd scarpered when I arrived to challenge him! He unlocked the door and ran out!'

'Amos –'

'That was the chunk I heard! It was the front door swinging shut!'

'First it's the till, now it's the door –'

'See for yourself, Mr Wilks,' Amos said magisterially, standing back. He gave the door a little push. It swung home into its lock with a chunk.

'Well, of course, if it was left open it would close with a chunk,' Henry began.

'Mr Wilks!' Amos said in an awful voice.

'Anybody can make a mistake, Amos –'

'In thirty years as an innkeeper, have I ever failed to lock up?'

'There's a first time for everything –'

'Not for things that never happen!'

'Look, Amos, it's nothing to be ashamed of. We all make mistakes –'

'Oh no! I locked that door. I bolted it. I always do. You know I do. Somebody's unlocked and unbolted it.' He opened the door, gestured out into the night air, and let the door swing shut. 'Opened the door, ran out, and the door came to after him.'

Henry considered him. He seemed absolutely certain sure about it ... Happen he oughtn't to dismiss it as just a fantasy. 'How did he get in, though?' he asked. 'If he walked out –'

'Ran out, Mr Wilks. I disturbed him –'

'I don't know so much. Takes a while to unfasten that door,

25

as Walter'll tell you when he's waiting outside with his tongue hanging out at opening time. If he was here, he walked out. But how did he get into the place?' Henry began to move about the empty bar room. 'No windows been forced?'

They made a tour. None of the windows showed any damage. Henry paused and half-turned to Amos. Amos said, in a tone of almost wild emphasis, 'There's been somebody here! I can sense it. And I locked that door.'

'I'm not accusing you, Amos—'

'You don't believe me!'

'I haven't said I don't—'

'So what'll we do?'

'Get back to bed.'

'Eh?' cried Amos.

'I'm dropping on my feet. I'm going back to bed.'

'Shouldn't we ring t'police?'

'What for?'

'To tell 'em we've been broken into?'

Henry took a moment before he replied. 'You ring 'em if you want to. Tell 'em we found t'front door unlocked, nowt gone, no damage to windows or owt like that. You ring 'em and say that.' He headed for the back of the bar and the stairs to his bedroom. 'Rather you than me,' he ended.

When he had gone, Amos stood for a long moment taking in his words. He tried to picture himself meeting Constable Dewes on the threshold, demonstrating the open doors and ... And what?

Hang it, t'police were there to protect you! Weren't they always saying they'd rather be called out on a wild goose chase than miss a chance to catch a villain? He marched to the phone.

With his hand upon it, he paused. The constable would come and find nothing. Word would get out, the way it always does. The customers would never let him forget it. 'Any burglars last night, Amos?' He could just imagine them ...

He took his hand away from the phone. He didn't want to be a laughing stock. It hurt his dignity.

He went back to the door, locked it, bolted it, put on the

chain – a thing he hadn't done for thirty years. He marched to the back door and made sure it was locked, the key safely hung on its hook below the shelf that held the few cookbooks and free pamphlets on cheese dishes and other goodies. He surveyed the door. After a moment he fetched a chair from the kitchen table and wedged it under the door handle. Better safe than sorry.

But he must get down first in the morning and take it away before Mr Wilks saw it.

He went into the bar for a last look round. 'All the same,' he said half-aloud, 'somebody's bin in here. I know it.'

He slept badly so had no trouble getting up ahead of Henry. He took the chair away from the door handle and, as an afterthought, undid the chain on the front door. No need to let Henry know he'd taken that extra precaution either.

The partners took it in turns to make breakfast, although it was understood that if one wanted smoked haddock while the other preferred bacon and sausage, each should cook his own. This morning it was Amos's turn. As Henry came in Amos said tersely over his shoulder: 'Eggs?'

'Aye,' said Henry, equally terse.

It was a rotten breakfast. There were no corn flakes in the packet, the tea tasted as if Amos had put in four spoonfuls each and ten for the pot, he burnt the toast, and to cap it all, the eggs were hard. Henry pushed back his chair and looked out, breathing in the cold damp air of the morning and thinking that, as if it wasn't bad enough to be dragged out of bed in the dark, at nine o'clock the sky still hadn't lightened. It was going to rain, that was certain; the twinge in his elbow told him so.

It rained. Henry waited until a quarter to ten, hoping it would stop, but by then he was at the end of his tether. Amos would hardly speak a word to him. Henry put on his mackintosh and his cap and marched out into the downpour, determined to get some exercise and some intelligent company.

When he reached Emmerdale on foot Joe was just nosing his car out of the farm lane into the road. In a box beside him was a load of tile pipes.

'Where you off to?'

'Clicker End. Water's collecting there.'

'Aye, I reckon everybody's having trouble wi' water in this weather.' Annie had often told him that her late husband Jacob had had a long-standing ambition to drain the Emmerdale land properly, but it had been left to Joe to achieve this. But even Joe was defeated by Clicker End. Henry stood back to let him drive on, but a glance in the rear mirror made Joe pause. A handsome Citröen went by.

Joe made no move to drive on. Henry looked at him in surprise. Joe said: 'That's the fourth time that chap's been past this morning.'

'Eh?'

'Last time, he came halfway into the yard. I was doing the drive.' Joe was trying to level out the potholes before the winter weather made them traps of mud or ice.

'What did he want?'

'Nowt, s'far as I could gather. I asked him if he was lost and he said no and backed out again.'

Henry frowned. 'Peculiar.'

'Aye.' Joe shrugged. 'Well, I must be off. I think you're in time for coffee.'

'I hope so,' Henry said piously, and hurried on.

A piece of Annie's dripping cake and a cup of coffee revived Henry. He told Annie about the disturbance of the previous night.

'And nothing was missing?' she asked.

'Not a thing. Amos is going around this morning like Sherlock Holmes only without the magnifying glass, but he couldn't see any gaps in the decor.'

They were still discussing it when Matt and Sam came in. Sam perked up his ears, but Matt was making too much noise washing his hands to catch the subject of conversation. He came on the scene when Sam was snorting that Amos always got up in the boughs about nowt and who would bother to rob the Woolpack, any road?

'Hey!' said Matt.

'What?'

'I saw somebody hurrying away from the Woolpack last night.'

'Well, there's nothing in that,' Henry pointed out. 'Most folk hurry home at turning out time.'

'But this was about one in the morning.'

There was a silence. Henry stared at Matt. It was impossible to disbelieve Matt. Amos could and would get things wrong, but never Matt.

'But it doesn't make sense,' Annie began. 'Nothing taken?'

'Well ... I never actually looked. I thought the thing was like television wrestling – all show and no blow. I left it to Amos. But he knows what should be in the place and he didn't report anything gone.'

'That's right peculiar,' Sam said.

'Aye.'

'It's a day for funny goings-on,' Henry remarked. 'Joe was just saying, a feller's driven past Emmerdale four times this morning.'

'Four times?' Sam scratched his head. 'Same feller as has been prowling at t'Woolpack?'

Henry thought about that but shook his head. 'Nay, a man with a car like that doesn't break into little country pubs.'

'I haven't seen him,' Matt said.

'Did Dolly, I wonder?'

'Dolly's not here. She decided not to stay overnight with us last night,' Annie explained. 'She brought some of her gear but when she unpacked it in her room found she'd left her nightdress and dressing-gown at the vicarage, so she went back there just for one more night. I offered her one of mine,' she added with a smile, 'but she didn't take me up.'

They talked on about the events until Matt had to get back to work. Sam returned to his carpentry; the 'lamb' was coming along nicely.

At opening time, however, curiosity drove him to put on his topcoat and walk down to the village for a pint at the Woolpack.

Dolly was getting the rough side of her employer's tongue this morning. She could do nothing right. When opening time came, she went to unlock the front door, where she could already hear Walter shuffling on the threshold.

'I'm the one who sees to the door, if you please, Miss Acaster,' Amos said, and swept her aside.

She served Walter his pint. A few more customers drifted in and were looked after by Amos. No young man came in with an eye for Dolly, he was glad to note. He thought with some resentment that Mr Wilks had vanished as usual – almost never around to help during midday opening hours, was Mr Wilks. What Mr Wilks would have found to do was unclear, since business was very slack – but that was beside the point.

Irritated, he turned to the bar – to find Miss Acaster removing the bottle from the dispenser labelled whisky.

'And what do you think you're doing?' he inquired.

'I'm getting another bottle for the dispenser,' she replied, surprised.

'And why, may I ask? Leave it alone.'

'But ... Mr Brearley ... it needs a new one.'

'Nothing of the kind, Miss Acaster.'

'But ...' She held out the bottle she'd removed. 'It's empty.'

The haughty tone fell away from Amos as his jaw fell open. 'Eh?' he said.

He took the bottle from her. It was undeniably empty. 'Well,' he said in a choked voice, 'that's proof. That's absolute proof someone was in here last night! For I put a full bottle up there myself at about nine o'clock, and we certainly didn't sell more than four whiskies after that!'

Mr Wilks returned home from his walk, somewhat cheered. The rain had stopped, his mac had dried off, he'd seen a red grouse, the world wasn't such a bad place after all. He walked into the Woolpack bar, determined to be nice to his partner.

'So there you are, Mr Wilks!' Amos cried, shaking an empty whisky bottle at him. 'Perhaps now you won't be so disbelieving!'

'Amos!' cried Henry, starting back. 'What's got into you? Can't come near you but you brandish a weapon!'

'This bottle, Mr Wilks, was more than two-thirds full last night when we went to bed. Miss Acaster will bear me out.'

Henry's intention to be humorous evaporated. He saw that Dolly was taking it quite seriously, and that meant is wasn't nonsense.

'You what?' he temporised.

'You didn't have a whisky in the middle of the night, did you, Mr Wilks?'

'I ... now Amos ... you know I wouldn't do a thing like that. If I did wake up and feel like a nip, I'd tell you. I ... let me see ... I had one last night just before we closed, and stood one to Isaac Plumley.'

'That's two,' Amos said. 'Did you sell any others?'

'Let me think. Early on ... aye ... The Pryors had one each ...'

'That's right,' Dolly agreed. 'About nine o'clock. That emptied the bottle and ... I remember now ... Mr Brearley put up a fresh one.'

'At nine o'clock,' Amos pointed out. 'And you had one with Mr Plumley at about ten-thirty. Who else served whisky between nine and ten-thirty?'

'You did, Mr Brearley,' prompted Dolly. 'Don't you remember? That little man asked you for a whisky and you tried to tell him he'd had enough already.'

'Aye,' Amos said, 'Him ... That's three from the new bottle. Three, sitha. At the most, four had gone from it. I remember noting the level when I was tidying up.'

'And what does it tell you, Amos?' Henry asked, a bit baffled.

'Someone was in here last night, Mr Wilks, drinking up our whisky after we closed.'

Part of this verdict was heard by a customer going out. 'Drinking after you've closed?' he called. 'You'll have the bobby after you.'

Sam passed him coming in. 'What's that about the bobby?' he inquired. 'You called him in about the break-in?'

'Not yet, but I'm going to,' Amos declared. 'That's evidence, is that! The whisky's gone. Between closing time last night and this minute, two-thirds of a bottle of whisky has vanished.'

'Vanished? How d'you mean?'

31

'It's gone. Somebody's drunk it.'

'But there wasn't a dirty glass anywhere around, Amos,' Henry objected.

Amos sniffed. 'Folks as'd burglarise a pub don't bother with glasses,' he remarked. 'They swig it from t'bottle.'

'And put the bottle back in the dispenser?'

That gave Amos pause. 'I . . . er . . .'

'I'll have a shandy, please, Amos,' Sam put in.

'Aye.' Automatically Amos got him his drink. His mind was still with the empty whisky bottle.

Dolly meanwhile was putting in a full bottle. Sam, taking his first sip, watched her, and then his eye as usual travelled up from the range of bottles to the shelf above.

'Hey!' he said.

Henry and Amos, about to address each other, turned to him in surprise.

In a low, stricken voice, Sam said: 'Where's t'Butterworth Ball?'

The silence that ensued was so intense that Dolly turned from her work to look at them. All three men were staring, aghast, at the niche on the shelves above the bar, where the trophy was kept.

It was empty.

'It's gone!' whispered Sam. 'What you done with it, Amos? You've no right to move it wi'out consulting me. I'm chairman of the cricket team –'

'I haven't touched it!' cried Amos, but in a whisper. 'I've not laid a finger on that ball since you put it there last summer.'

'By heaven!' murmured Henry. 'Dolly, when you dusted this morning – didn't you notice it was gone?'

'I didn't do the shelves this morning, Mr Wilks. I did them yesterday. I have to get a stool to get up there, so I only do them every second day.'

'And was it there yesterday?'

'Of course,' she said. She never actually touched the Butterworth Ball, understanding that this sacred relic must not be handled by the unworthy. She only ever flicked it with a

32

duster. But it had certainly been there to be flicked yesterday morning.

'There,' groaned Amos. 'I told you so!'

Henry eyed him. Typical! Only a man like Amos would say 'I told you so!' 'What did you tell me?' he inquired, with some acidity.

'I told you someone had been in here last night!'

'As I recall, you took a good look round and said nothing was missing. Now it's two-thirds of a bottle of whisky and the Butterworth Ball.'

'Amos, Amos,' moaned Sam. 'Why didn't you report this last night?'

'I didn't notice it last night –'

'Didn't notice it? Didn't notice that it was gone?'

'Well ... I ... I expected if anything was took, it'd be something valuable –'

'And you think t'Butterworth Ball's not valuable?'

Amos went pink. He knew he had blundered. 'I ... er ... I only mean, in money terms, Mr Pearson. A burglar, you know ... you'd reckon he'd take things he could sell for money. To a fence, you know,' he added, dredging up the word from some crime reports he'd read.

'Can't imagine a fence giving anybody much for an old cricket ball,' Dolly remarked with unfeeling common sense.

Sam eyed her fresh, bright face and her untroubled blue eyes with dismay. This – *this*! – was the girl who was to move into the farm this very day. One who didn't understand the value of the Butterworth Ball.

Henry, seeing the expression on Sam's face, put in quickly, 'She's right, you know, Sam. I can understand an intruder quaffing the whisky. But why should he want the Butterworth Ball?'

No one could suggest an explanation. Sam took a gulp of his shandy. Understanding or inspiration came to him as he swallowed. He began to cough. 'It's them!' he cried. 'Them!'

'Who?' exclaimed Henry. 'Who, them?'

'Them Robblesfield lot! They've stolen t'Ball!'

'Robblesfield?' said Dolly.

33

'They never agreed with umpire's decision in last summer's match,' Sam plunged on. 'They allus said we should have lost, and they should've got t'Ball –'

'But surely they wouldn't break in and –'

'Now wait a minute, wait a minute,' Henry said, trying to keep his head. 'Nobody broke in.'

'Mr Wilks, I tell you, I know somebody was in here last night!'

'But the door was locked – you said so yourself. And none of the windows was forced.'

'That's as may be, but ...'

'It's them,' Sam insisted. 'The Robblesfield lot!'

'You can't go accusing folk without evidence, Sam –'

'Henry, I know that lot! They've taken t'Ball.'

'But why?'

'To show us up, that's why!'

'But who notices the Ball?' Dolly put in.

Sam glared. 'I just did, didn't I? And anybody else with any feeling for Beckindale'd notice its disappearance.'

'Oh,' groaned Amos. 'Oh, dear, and I had it in my keeping!'

Sam shook his head. 'Amos,' he said, 'you've let us down.'

Amos, a broken man, had nothing to say in his own defence. Dolly said, woman-like, 'But it's only an old cricket ball.'

'I've just told you –'

'Nay, wait a minute, Mr Pearson. I mean, the Butterworth Ball actually is an old cricket ball. I've dusted it often enough so I should know. It just sits there. Nobody touches it. Nobody even goes close.'

'But you don't understand –'

'Hang on, Sam,' Henry said. He gave Dolly a grateful nod. 'You've got something there. Sam, the Butterworth Ball sits up there in its niche. What does it look like from where you're standing?'

'It looks like a cricket ball, of course,' Sam said with indignation. And then, light dawning: 'Just like any old cricket ball!'

'Exactly!'

'Eeh,' said the old man. 'I've got another just like it in

34

my shed at t'farm. From this distance, nobody'd ever know the difference.'

'There you are,' said Dolly.

Sam glanced at her. There was good in that girl, you had to admit. Quick wits, intelligence ... And she had the good of the village at heart.

'The honour of Beckindale will be intact,' Sam said. 'I'll go right back and fetch that ball – and let's hope nobody from Robblesfield comes in to take a look at that niche while I'm gone!'

He hastened away. Old Walter, who'd been a baffled witness of this muted drama, watched him go. He waved his tankard at Dolly, who hurried to get him a refill. While her back was turned the door opened and a young man, very well-dressed and with that well-barbered, well-manicured air that bespeaks money, came in.

'I'll have a half of real ale, please,' he said.

'Right away, sir,' Dolly said, and turned to put Walter's drink before him.

She was at once face to face with the newcomer. Her hand suddenly trembled so much that she slopped half of Walter's beer over the counter. Walter made a sound of protest. She brought the tankard back and added more to the pull to bring it to the top again.

'Hello, Dolly,' said the young man. 'To coin a phrase.'

She said nothing.

'Surprised?'

No words would come. She stared at him.

'Sorry to bring about the reunion in public. But this seemed the only place where I could catch up with you.'

'How did you find me?' she asked at last, speaking as if in pain.

'It took some doing.'

They stood face to face, the bar top between them. Amos, still arguing with Henry about the niche without its Ball, half-turned in her direction to see what she was about.

'Half of real ale,' she said, and moved to get it.

'Dolly,' he said pleadingly.

'Go away,' she whispered. 'Go away. Leave me alone.'

He shook his head. 'Never again, Dolly. Not now I've found you again.'

Tears were sparkling at the rims of her eyes. 'Richard,' she said, carefully placing the half-pint before him, 'for pity's sake, drink this and go.'

He took the tankard, went to a table, set it down, pulled out a chair, and settled himself. 'When do you finish work now?' he called.

Amos looked round, surprised. Why, it was that young man again, the one who'd been in yesterday. Making a move towards striking up a friendship, by the sound of it. He glanced at Dolly to see how she was responding. If she was being too forward, he'd have to speak to her.

He needn't have worried. On Dolly's face he saw reluctance and despair, but no welcome of any kind.

CHAPTER THREE

Sam Pearson smuggled the cricket ball into the Woolpack without being observed. He would have preferred to put it in its niche himself, but that might attract attention. Under his supervision Amos was allowed to do it. Once there it looked like the Butterworth Ball.

But it was a lie, and Sam knew it. He accepted a shandy on the house from Henry, having left most of the one he ordered earlier on, and while he drank it he looked at the ball. How could it be that he, Sam Pearson, was taking part in a deception?

Troubled by his conscience, he turned towards the church when he left the inn. It never did any harm to ask the Almighty's forgiveness for something that didn't seem quite honest.

The vicar was pottering about the parish church when he went in. He nodded to Sam but made no attempt to speak to him when he saw the old man take a seat and bend his head on to his hand in prayer. Mr Hinton was putting putty in a crack round one of the brass plaques erected in memory of a soldier killed in the Boer War. No one else these days remained to care for it, but Mr Hinton felt it ought not to be neglected.

When Sam got up, the vicar was standing back to admire his handiwork. 'How are you, Mr Pearson?' he inquired gently.

'Well enough, vicar, thank'ee. Yourself?'

'Oh, I'm fine, thanks,' He yawned suddenly. 'Oh, sorry. A little short on sleep, I'm afraid.'

'What's the matter? Bed at t'vicarage not comfy? If not, I daresay Annie could discuss –'

'No, no, the bed's fine, thank you. It's just that I retired rather late, and just when I'd dropped off I was roused by some kind of commotion in the lane.'

'Eh?' said Sam.

'Someone running, I think. I got the impression he was coming to the vicarage ... Silly, of course.'

'That's odd, though, vicar. What time was that?'

'Just after one, I think.' Mr Hinton looked apologetic. 'I get interested in what I'm reading and forget to go to bed, you see.'

Sam looked as if he found that hard to understand. Years of early-to-bed, early-to-rise had made him consider it practically a sin to be up after about ten. But he had more important matters on his mind.

'Did you come down to the door?' he asked.

'No, I waited for a ring at the bell but no one came. So I realised it was probably just some youngster going home in a hurry after a party.'

'Mm ...' said Sam. From what Henry said, he and Amos had been disturbed around one in the morning by sounds downstairs. And now the Butterworth Ball was gone. But anybody going back to Robblesfield wouldn't go past the vicarage. On the other hand, anybody going to Robblesfield would almost certainly have a car – so perhaps the car had been parked at lane-top.

'Did you hear a car afterwards?' he inquired.

'After what?'

'After the footsteps in the lane.'

'I'm not aware that I did,' said the vicar, a bit surprised. Really, it was very good of Mr Pearson to be so concerned about the matter.

'You heard someone going by on foot – that's all?'

'I ... er ... don't really recall. I was awakened, you see, out of my first sleep. I don't really know what roused me. Then I half-got up, thinking someone was coming up the path. I waited for the bell to ring but it didn't. Then I realised the sound I'd heard must have been someone hurrying – loudly – up the lane.' Hinton smiled. 'It's not much of a drama, really.'

'Happen,' Sam said. He just wished the vicar had gone to the door, or looked out the window. Mind you, it had been a moonless night. Not much to see out of a window. Still, it might have helped.

Helped in what way, he asked himself, as he took his leave. Even if he could prove that one of the Robblesfield team had hurried up Vicarage Lane last night, what good did that do?

When he got home, dinner was already on the table and his daughter wasn't best pleased at his dilly-dallying. In fact, there seemed to be a strange atmosphere at Emmerdale altogether. It should have been a lively afternoon, for Dolly was moving in. But though she made two trips with Matt to fetch her belongings, and though Annie tried her best to make everything welcoming, Dolly seemed very subdued.

'We have us teas about five-thirty,' Annie explained. 'You'll want a bite earlier than that because you'll be opening up at t'Woolpack –'

'It's all right,' Dolly broke in. 'I don't usually bother much.'

'But you must eat,' Annie rebuked her. 'What about dinner-time? Do you eat then?'

'Mr Wilks usually makes an opportunity for me to sit down to something in the back room. We're not usually so busy at dinnertime.'

'Hm,' Annie said. Was that why she seemed pale and rather listless today? Was she in need of nourishment? If so, it would be easy enough to remedy at Emmerdale.

She noticed that Matt was stealing occasional worried glances at Dolly. So, she herself wasn't the only one who thought something was wrong.

But there was little opportunity to pursue the matter because surprisingly quickly it was time for the girl to get back to the Woolpack. Today was Saturday, always the busiest day of the week. Annie set out cold meat and pickle for her but Dolly simply pushed the food around on her plate before springing up and saying she must be off.

As they listened to her scooter fading into the distance, Annie and Matt exchanged a look. But neither could think of how to express the strange feeling they had that Dolly was in distress.

Sam went to the Woolpack after tea to keep watch for Robblesfield men come to crow over the loss of the Butterworth Ball. But to his mystification, no one appeared. His grandson Joe had headed for a more lush setting tonight – he had taken Lesley Gibson out to dinner at the Bear and Staff on the River Lill. They'd had a good meal of the old-fashioned English kind, and now were amusing themselves with a game of darts in the bar.

Joe was trying for a treble top when Harry Teaker got in his way.

''Lo, Joe,' he said, in a muzzy voice, weaving a little on his feet.

'Hello, Little.'

'What you doing here?'

'Playing darts,' Joe said, stepping round him to take aim. 'What are *you* doing here?'

'Drinking,' said Little Teaker, eyeing Lesley with open admiration. 'Aren't you going to introduce me?'

With a sigh Joe did so. 'This is Miss Gibson. Harry Teaker is the demon bowler of Robblesfield – known as Little Teaker.'

'Nothing to do with my size,' the other explained carefully.

'It was just that, as a lad I had a big brother.'

'How d'you do,' Lesley said nonchalantly, accepting the darts from Joe.

'I bet you hit more than just a dartboard,' Little said in admiration. 'Fellers dropping at your feet, eh?'

'By the dozen,' Lesley agreed, otherwise ignoring him as she sighted for her shot.

'I must hear more of this. I'll bring my friend over ... Buy you a drink.' Weaving his way across the room, Little Teaker was lost to view.

Lesley threw her first dart then turned to raise an eyebrow at Joe. 'Is he a friend of yours?'

'Are you kidding? Didn't I tell you that us Beckindalers are at daggers drawn with the men of Robblesfield?'

'No, but really ...'

'He's not as bad as he sounds,' Joe soothed. 'Just takes a drop too much. Doesn't know when to stop.'

'He gets more attractive by the minute.'

'No, he's all right really. Gets a bit fed up because his brother has all the say-so in the business, but Little has his good points.'

Little reappeared at that moment, followed by a pretty girl in a soft wool dress that clung at all the right places. 'Now then,' he said in an important tone, 'this is Lily ... You sit here, Lily.' He pushed her into a chair at a nearby table. 'That's Miss Gibson, a friend of my friend Joe. What you all having? Yours is a pint, Joe, and Lily's a snowball, I know. What about you, Miss Gibson?'

'Get you!' mocked Lily. 'Miss Gibson!'

'My ole friend Joe has not feen sit – par'me, not seen fit to tell me the lady's first name. Isn't that right, Miss Gibson dear lady?'

'It's Lesley,' said Lesley, looking as if she felt she could willingly throw the darts at Little Teaker rather than the board.

'There y'are! Knew I'd get a proper introduction sooner or later. What you drinking? I know, though – classy, you are – you're the sort that likes Campari and soda, eh, like th skinny girl on telly.'

'No, thanks, I –'

'Ne'er mind,' Little interrupted, 'I'll get you something nice.' He turned to go, then paused. 'Rather have a touch of the hard stuff, Joe?'

'No, thanks, I'm driving. In fact, half of ale will be enough, ta.'

'Lily drives,' Little said. 'Great gal, Lily. So I'll have my usual, eh? A double scotch. Be a minute.' He made off.

Everyone exchanged embarrassed little smiles. 'Great,' said Lily. 'Every time he takes me out he gets legless. He knows I hate driving his rotten car, especially at night on these country roads.'

'I know what you mean,' Lesley said. 'I won't bring my car out of town. I need lamp-posts and traffic lights.'

Little came back. 'Waiter's bringing 'em. Thought I better not hang about. Lily gets impatient.'

'Well!' she exclaimed.

'What's to do, then?' Little continued, ignoring her. 'How's Beckindale, Joe? How's old Sam?'

'All right,' Joe said, a bit surprised. 'Keeps going, tha knows.'

'Aye, keeps going. When the others have stopped. Famous, is that. Famous funny cartoon. D'you ever see it? Feller in an orchestra still tootling and ... But that's not what I wanted to tell you, Joe. A real funny story ...' Little had reached over to emphasize his point and in so doing had innocently dropped his hand on Lesley's knee.

Lesley got up so suddenly that Little slipped forward, almost bumping his chin on the table.

'Sorry,' Joe said, 'we've got to be going.' He had risen with Lesley.

'But you haven't had your drinks yet –'

'You drink 'em,' said Joe, leading Lesley away.

'Don't,' said Lily to their retreating backs, 'he's quite likely to do it!'

Lesley looked over her shoulder. 'Nice to have met you,' she said, pointedly ignoring Little.

41

Lily waved.

'Stuck up,' mumbled her escort. 'That's what she is. Stuck up.'

'She just has a proper respect for herself,' said Lily with asperity. 'Time I developed that.'

'You ... You're all right, Lily. You don't walk away when I'm trying to tell you something.'

'Not so far. But the day will come ...'

'Pity they didn't stop. I was going to tell them something they'd have liked to hear. I bet they're searching everywhere for it.'

'For what?' she asked, leaning back to let the waiter set down the drinks. She saw with amusement that Little had ordered Pimms for Lesley.

'The Butterworth Ball.'

'What's the Butterworth Ball when it's at home?'

'There, you see?' he said. 'That's the whole point. It's not at home. It's gone, and I know where it is ...'

'Bully for you.'

'It's a good story, Lily. Make you laugh. Come on, drink up. Mustn't waste it, eh? Waste not, want not.'

Joe, unaware that he had missed a chance to solve the mystery that was making life a misery for his grandfather, took Lesley to finish the evening at Demdyke Row. When they parted at last, Beckindale was silent and all its inhabitants asleep.

But at Emmerdale two people were wakeful. Annie was sitting up in her bed listening in distress to the sound she could hear coming from the attic bedroom given over to Dolly.

Up there in the dark, Dolly was sobbing her heart out.

Next day Annie reproached herself with having done nothing about it. There had been a human soul in need last night and she had simply stayed in her own room, listening and worrying. Yet she felt she didn't know Dolly well enough yet to interfere. She wished they were better acquainted. This Sunday morning she seemed totally without her usual buoyant good humour.

The Emmerdale family went to church as usual. Mr Hin

ton delayed Annie and her father for a discussion about the Christmas trees needed for the parish church and the church hall. Dolly strolled on with Matt.

'Everything all right?' he asked, drawing her arm through his.

'Fine, thanks.'

'Only ... if you think you're not going to like Emmerdale, you only have to say. Ma wouldn't hold it against you.'

'It's not *that*,' she cried.

'Well, what?' There was nothing accusatory in his tone; he simply wanted to know, so he could help.

'It's nothing, really, Matt. Nothing important.'

He let it go for the moment. They made their way down the path through the churchyard and came out by the lych-gate into the lane.

Here a handsome Citroen car was parked. Dolly, who had never seen it before, walked towards it without concern. A man got out and came towards her. Matt felt Dolly tremble and falter to a stop.

'Oh, God, no ...' he heard her murmur.

Astounded at the despair in her voice, he gazed at the man confronting them now.

'Good morning,' said the stranger. 'I'm Richard Roper.'

'Morning.' Matt said.

'Coming?' Richard said to Dolly.

'Coming? Where?' she gasped.

'To lunch, of course. That's what we arranged.'

'No we didn't –'

'Why else would I book a table? Come on, Dolly, don't be temperamental –'

'Excuse me,' Matt said, speaking with a crispness not usual with him, 'I think Dolly has arrangements of her own.'

'She's got an arrangement with me. Haven't you, darling?'

'Please,' she whispered. 'Please, Richard ...'

'I've booked at the Red Lion, Brassington. It's quite a drive. We don't want to be late.'

'Just a minute –'

'No, Matt wait.' Dolly disengaged her arm from Matt's. She

43

moved a little way towards the car. 'Richard, go and wait in the car for me. I'll join you there.'

He eyed her. He was wary, but already a dawning triumph was in his brown eyes. 'All right, but don't be long.'

He strolled away. There was something very proprietorial in his air. Dolly had turned back to Matt so didn't see it, but Matt was struck by it.

'Look, you don't have to go just because he booked a table –'

'I'd better go, Matt. It would only cause an unpleasantness otherwise –'

'But that's blackmail,' Matt said, his blunt features creasing in a frown.

'No, I did say I'd see him today, to talk things over.'

'Things?'

'I'll explain later.' She clearly didn't want a public scene. She particularly didn't want a scene that would involve Matt. 'I must go.'

'But there's a rehearsal this afternoon, Dolly –'

'I'll be there, Matt. I promise.'

'Wouldn't you rather just come to the Woolpack, as we'd intended –'

'Nay, I'd best go with Richard. You'll understand by and by.'

White and strained, her face spoke of a misery she wouldn't express. He let her go because to go on protesting only made things worse for her.

As she got into the car, Annie joined Matt. She drew up in astonishment. 'Is that Dolly going?'

'Aye. His name's Richard Roper.'

'But I thought we were going to the Woolpack for a sherry?'

'Seems not, Ma.'

'Who's Richard Roper?'

He shrugged.

Behind them, Sam was to be heard laying down the law about overwintering begonias to Docky Beeton. Quickly before he joined them, Annie said, 'Matt, something's really wrong. Dolly's very unhappy.'

'Aye.'

'Last night ... I heard her crying.'

He turned to her with a sharp movement. 'I didn't hear her?'

'Nay, lad, if you had...? I didn't know what to do myself, and I couldn't have gone to her without it being embarrassing ... you know ...'

He nodded. Sam dropped into step with them. 'I've told him a thousand times the roots got to be kept from damp or they'll go mouldy,' he remarked. 'But some folk never learn. Hey-up, where's Dolly?'

'She had to go somewhere.'

'What? But I thought she was going to t'Woolpack –'

'Something came up, Dad.'

'Oh, if she would rather go off on her own –'

'Now Dad, it can't be much of a treat for Dolly to have a drink in t'Woolpack when she works there every day.'

Sam raised his eyebrows. 'Now that's true. I never thought o' that. Aye, of course. I should ha' thought. A gradely lass like Dolly wouldn't back out of a date without a good reason.'

Unaware of the constraint on his daughter and Matt, Sam talked on cheerfully until they reached the Woolpack. There they found Joe, already settled with a half and looking as if he had no quarrel with the world. He rose quickly to order for them as they came in. 'Cider for you, Grandad? Or shandy?'

'Cider, thanks, Joe.'

'Sherry for Ma, pint for Matt. Here, where's Dolly? I thought she was coming?'

'Huh,' sniffed Amos, pouring sherry. 'Prefers to be off with yon chap in his flashy car.'

'Up to her, that is,' Matt said.

'Cheers,' said Joe, handing him his pint, which Henry had drawn.

'Oh, aye, true enough, it's up to her. And of course once I realised they were old friends I had no objections to them making a date.'

Annie said to Henry, 'I see you've got your tree up, Henry.' Her glance said, 'Talk to me about the tree.'

'Yes, handsome, isn't it? Dolly hasn't finished decorating it yet –'

'Nor will, if she keeps going gallivanting,' remarked Amos. 'But her free time's her own, naturally. And she'd have to give him some attention, being they're like engaged.'

Matt stiffened. Joe said, 'Who's engaged?' Henry, catching on too late that he should have avoided mentioning Dolly, groaned inwardly. Amos said, 'Them. That feller and Miss Acaster.'

'Dolly's engaged?' Sam said in amazement.

Rather pleased with the sensation he'd caused, Amos nodded. 'She mentioned it to me once, in the course of conversation.'

'She never mentioned it to me,' Annie said.

'Well, you're not her employer, Mrs Sugden, now are you?' He looked at her rather anxiously. 'Sherry to your liking?'

'It's fine, thanks, Amos.' She took her glass to a table at the other side of the room. Matt hesitated, divided between politeness and a wish to stay near Amos to find out what he could about Dolly. But other customers called him away, and Joe on an impulse of kindness invited Matt to throw a few darts. 'Pay no heed to Amos,' he murmured. 'You know he always gets everything wrong.'

Henry poured himself a scotch and went to join Annie. 'It's not good, Annie,' he said. 'This young man was in here yesterday – I arrived late on the scene but apparently he'd made himself quite at home. He acted as if he owned Dolly. I've never seen her so at a loss.'

Annie unbuttoned her tweed coat. The bar was warm. Yet she felt a chill – a chill of concern for Matt. Why should this happen to Matt? Hadn't he suffered enough? Just as he found someone he might care for, it turned out she was engaged to someone else.

'He came and collected her from church,' she said. 'I only saw the back of him, but Matt was right upset. I can't understand why she went –'

'I think she's afraid of him,' Henry said.

46

She looked up. 'Afraid?'

'Of the damage he can do. I don't know why. I don't know what's behind it. But I'll tell thee summat, Annie – I've been in business all my life and I know a wrecker when I see one. And that lad is a wrecker.'

She was silent. Across the room Matt was standing by while Joe played his darts. There was something so dependable, so calm and steady about Matt.

'It's a pity they hadn't got further on,' she murmured. 'Matt and Dolly. But it hadn't grown strong enough for her to confide in him yet. And now . . .'

'Now it's too late, happen.'

'Don't say that, Henry.'

'But it's true. And in a way, it's Matt's fault. He won't move on his own behalf. He's too modest to think she cares about him.' Henry sighed and tugged at his moustache. The fault was exactly the opposite of his own. He himself always moved too fast. Matt moved too slow. Somewhere, he thought, there had to be a happy medium.

Joe was trying to amuse Matt with an account of his meeting with Little Teaker last night. 'Half seas over, as usual these days,' he said. 'A good man gone wrong there.'

'Aye.'

'He had a real pretty girl with him. Don't know why she puts up wi' him. You should have seen him – trying to make an impression on Lesley.'

'Put your nose out of joint, did he?'

'No fear.' Thinking that he ought not to dwell on his own successes in the circumstances, Joe went on: 'I don't suppose Little will be bowling for them next season if he goes on the way he is. He won't be able to see where he's aiming.'

'Next season?' his grandfather put in, catching the word although in the midst of a conversation with Docky Beeton. He came to join them. 'Don't talk about next season,' he groaned. 'We got to find that ball before next season or we won't be able to play the match.'

'All the better,' muttered Joe, thinking of the plotting and counter-plotting that had gone on last summer.

'What d'you mean? It's traditional, that match. Tradition's important –'

'Listen, Grandad,' Joe put in, to forestall a lecture on Beckindale traditions, 'I think I know how the thief got in and took the Butterworth Ball.'

'What?'

'I think I know how it was done.'

'How? What's the solution?' Sam beckoned to Amos with his cider glass. 'Amos, come and listen to this – Joe thinks he knows how you-know-what was done.'

Amos hurried to join them. A sleepless night last night had resulted in no useful thoughts on his part.

'I think,' Joe said, 'that the thief never had to break in.'

'Now, Joe, I've told Mr Wilks and I'll tell you. I locked and bolted that door –'

'I'm sure you did, Amos. But you locked and bolted it with the thief on the inside.'

'What?'

'I think he hid in the Woolpack while you were still open, and came out after you'd locked up and gone to bed.'

'Never!' cried Amos. 'Where would he have hidden?'

'In the loo, happen.'

'Nowt o't'sort! I allus look in the toilets – and I get Dolly to look in t'ladies.'

'Get on wi' thee,' snorted Sam. 'If anybody wanted to hide, there's a thousand places in this old building they could do it.'

'I tell you, Sam Pearson, I search the premises every night. A licensee has responsibilities, tha knows. Cellars full of intoxicating liquors ... Of course I search before I lock up.'

'Hey,' said Joe. 'You say you look in the gents, and Dolly looks in the ladies?'

'Aye, that's right.'

'Simultaneously?'

'What?'

'Do you go and look in the gents same time as Dolly looks in t'other?'

'Well ... I couldn't quite say ... I suppose ... Happen we don't coincide completely ...'

48

'There you are then.'

'Where are we?' asked Sam.

'What's to stop a feller from hiding in the gents while Dolly looks in the ladies, and nipping out to hide in there while Amos looks in the gents?'

'I don't follow that,' Amos said, furrowing his brow.

'Dolly has to leave the premises – right? So goes and finishes her last-minute chores, looking in the ladies room, comes back putting her coat on and saying "All serene, Mr Brearley".'

'Well . . . more or less.'

'You're not going anywhere so last thing, before you lock up for the night, you go and have a look in the gents. Right?'

'Yes.'

'So this character is in the gents at the time Dolly looks in the ladies cloakroom. When he hears her go, he nips out and crosses the passage *from* the gents *to* the ladies. Then you go –'

'And look in the gents,' Sam joined in in chorus, 'and all the time he's in the ladies.'

Amos caught hold of his mutton-chops, one in each hand. 'Good gracious,' he said. 'Oh, heck!'

'So he never forced any windows. Didn't have to. He probably had a little kip until you'd settled down for the night. Then he comes out –'

'Takes Butterworth Ball –' said Sam, frowning.

'Drinks off the whisky,' said Amos with disapproval.

'Unbolts and unlocks the door, and walks out.'

'Well!'

'One of the Robblesfield team,' said Sam. 'And they'll be here to triumph over us before long, you mark my words! By heaven, what a disappointment it'll be to them when they find the ball is safe in place!'

Joe grinned and bowed, excusing himself to rejoin Matt. But Matt had quietly slipped out, preferring to be on his own for a bit. His thoughts were with Dolly. What was going on between her and that strange, sharp, handsome young man?

He was right in guessing there was no enjoyment in the encounter. Dolly had gone with Richard with the greatest reluctance, and though she had sat down at table with him, she had eaten not a morsel.

'What's the point, my darling, of ordering a first class meal if you don't attempt to try it?' he said in reproach.

'What's the point in us being here at all, Richard? I only came because you wouldn't take no for an answer.'

'I've taken too many denials. The time's come for everything to start going right for me.'

'Oh, Richard!'

'Don't you understand I never wanted things to be the way they were? I wanted us to stay together –'

'But you made no attempt to protect our relationship.'

'I did! I argued and argued –'

'With your mother?' She smiled sadly. 'Don't you see, that's what was wrong from the beginning. You never seemed to see that you don't argue about things like that. If it's important enough, you *act*.'

He summoned the waiter to take away their plates. Dolly shook her head when he asked if she would have a sweet. 'Just coffee, then,' he ordered. 'And I'll have a brandy. You, Dolly?'

'No thanks.'

'No, I remember, you never cared much for drink. Odd that you should make a career in licensing.'

She met his eyes. 'That was because accommodation usually goes with a job like that. And I needed somewhere to live.'

He coloured. 'There was no need for that. You didn't have to run away as if I would put you in chains –'

'You had me in chains, Richard! You kept me tied to you by saying you needed me –'

'I did need you, Dolly. I still need you.'

'Really?' There was a hardness in her tone. 'Well, there was a time when I needed *you*, Richard. If you'd really cared for me, I could have depended on you. But no. Mummy had said I was the wrong girl for you – not suitable to be the wife of a man with so much money, so many good connections –'

'She'd have got over that. I told you you only had to be patient –'

'Patient? More than three years' worth of patience? When

50

was she going to allow me inside her house – when I had grey hairs and a stoop?'

'Dolly, that's all in the past now. I've made up my own mind –'

'Too late, Richard. If you had done that two and a half years ago, and come to me ...' She hesitated, her voice almost broke. 'How happy I would have been! I can't tell you!'

'So you did love me,' he said. 'And you love me still.'

'No.'

'You do. You wouldn't be so upset over seeing me again,' he reasoned, 'if it didn't mean a lot to you.'

'No, Richard.'

The waiter came with the coffee. She sat back, clasping and unclasping her hands in her lap. The waiter poured from the clever little glass pot. She raised her tiny cup to her lips, eager for its bitter reviving flavour.

Richard sipped his brandy. He was watching her with the shrewd, intent expression of a leopard watching a doe. He had had a long search before he tracked her down to Emmerdale, but it had been worth it. She was still as vibrant, as desirable. She could still restore the meaning to his life, if he played his cards right.

He would have been the first to admit, self-deprecatingly, that he had been spoiled. The Ropers were a very wealthy family, with property here and there in most of the big cities, and farmland in South Africa. He, as the only son, had had everything he wanted in life – until he met Dolly.

He met her, of all places, on a beach at St Anne's. She had just come out of the sea, her swimsuit clinging to her lithe figure, her hair damp where the cap had not been able to protect it. He had just left a boring party in a house belonging to friends. He'd picked Dolly up as an antidote to boredom.

He made a date with her for that evening, never intending to turn up. But his mother was in one of her 'isn't-it-time-you-did-something-with-your-life-dear' moods, and he was driven to escape. Once out, he thought he might as well go to collect the pretty slender girl in the dark red swimsuit.

To his chagrin, she wasn't at the meetingplace. He couldn't

51

believe it. No one had ever stood him up before.

That afternoon on the beach she'd spoken to a group nearby, calling out, 'I'll see you back at the Collworth.' He went into a phone booth, looked it up, and found it to be a hotel in a quiet road to the north of the town. He drove there, and sent in word that he was waiting.

She came out, laughing and embarrassed. She was clad in a plain little blue print dress, her brown legs bare.

'Why weren't you at the cinema?' he demanded.

'But I didn't think you meant it,' she replied.

'Of course I meant it.'

She blushed, but stood her ground. 'No you didn't. You didn't have the least intention of really turning up.'

'How can you say that? I wouldn't have made a date if I didn't intend to keep it.'

'If you'd really meant it,' she said with a little laugh, 'you'd have asked which cinema. There's more than one.'

'Oh.' He was taken aback, but rallied, 'You should have told me so. How was I to know?'

She allowed him to persuade her she was in the wrong, and that was a preview of how their relationship was to develop. Whenever she asked to meet his parents, he put her off. When she wanted to know if they were heading for marriage or not, he told her it was too early to say. The months went by, and they grew more and more in love, but there was always something almost make-believe about it.

The reason was that he refused to face the facts. Dolly came from a very ordinary background, not at all like the girls from Roedean paraded before him by his mother. Mrs Roper wanted him to marry, but she wanted a 'suitable' daughter-in-law. He knew very well that she would never accept Dolly. Why, even her name was wrong. When he spoke of her to his mother he called her Dorothy. He couldn't face the prospect of marrying without his mother's approval, yet he kept on assuring Dolly they were going to get married. He just kept on thinking that one day, one day, everything would come right, as if by magic.

Dolly said to him, with total seriousness: 'When are you

going to grow up, Richard?'

He laughed. 'You mean you think I'm too boyish?'

'I'm serious. The word I'd use is immature, not boyish.'

'Dolly!'

She burst out, 'I can't go on like this! It's only half a life. I'm married to you but I'm not married. I'm not to see anyone else but you go away and leave me for ages at a time. Life's slipping away from me. It's like a dream or a trance I'm in. I can't go on any more!'

It was so unlike her. She was generally so bright, so capable. He tried to calm her, and then when she insisted that he must decide what he really wanted – marriage or his mother's approval – he grew angry. They had a great row that muttered on into the next day. He stalked out saying, 'Well, I'm going home – I'm expected at a dinner party. Try to be more agreeable when I get back.'

'There you are,' she flashed. 'You're going home. This isn't home. That's the truth of it.'

'Don't be silly. It's only a way of speaking.'

'A way of speaking the truth.'

'I'll see you tomorrow, Dolly.'

But when tomorrow came and he went back to soothe her down, she was gone.

He had been so angry at her 'desertion' at first that he'd put her right out of his mind. Besides, when his mother found out what had happened she was so pleased with him for breaking up that unsuitable relationship that he had basked in her approval unthinkingly. Yet though he'd intended to settle down and be the kind of son Mrs Roper wanted, he'd found it impossible. The girls she set before him seemed insipid compared with Dolly.

As time went by, an emptiness began to loom before him. He had known love. He couldn't settle for less. When he told her now he needed her, it was the simple truth. He couldn't fill the emptiness if she wasn't there.

'You and I can rebuild everything the way it used to be,' he said to her, leaning across to take her hand.

But she eluded his touch. 'You're like a little boy asking

53

to have his castle of bricks put together again,' she sighed. 'It's not possible. Nothing can ever be exactly the way it used to be. And besides ... I've changed, Richard.'

'Not that much. I won't believe that.'

'Whether you believe it, it's true. I'm not the Dolly Acaster you used to know.'

'But you couldn't have changed that much –'

'Oh yes I could. Life has changed me. This place has changed me.'

'This place? You mean – the village – that farm?' He hesitated. 'That chap who tried to act the champion – is he important?'

'Don't let's discuss him. Matt's part of the life here ... You wouldn't understand.'

'I think I could hold my own against that kind of opposition,' he said, with a thin smile.

'There!' she cried. 'You think it's some sort of game! You simply don't understand. It's not a team game, there's no score! There's no "opposition" – only people. People can be hurt, Richard, and I won't deny you're an expert at that. So go away. Go away and hurt people who know how to protect themselves from the likes of you.'

'I'm not going away.'

'Then I'll go.' She rose.

'I won't let you go, you know.'

She signalled to the waiter that she needed her coat. 'You still haven't grown up, Richard, have you? "It's mine, I want it!"'

'I need you.'

'We all need somebody. But it doesn't have to be me.'

'It does, Dolly. I know that now.'

She moved towards the man holding out her coat.

'Too bad,' she said. 'Because I've learned not to need you.'

CHAPTER FOUR

Amos said: 'I'm not saying owt against her, Mr Wilks. You're taking me up wrong. All I'm saying is, that young man, Mr Roper it is, you can see he's got money. Now can't you? I mean, that wrist watch ...'

'Oh aye,' Henry said. 'Seiko, is that. And his suit's Savile Row. But Dolly isn't the kind to be impressed by that.'

Amos, who was, shrugged expressively. 'It counts, say what you like. I mean, she can look at it this way. She can stay a bar person, with no great prospects, or she can wed Mr Roper and have everything the heart can desire.' He savoured the phrase, he being a writer. 'All the heart can desire ... aye.'

'But Dolly's heart doesn't desire money, happen. Seems to me it's Matt she wants.'

'But Matt's been married,' Amos said, as if that put paid to the notion of a second attempt.

'Amos,' Henry said, beginning to clear the breakfast things, 'I sometimes envy you. With your limited outlook, you can see little to get perturbed about.'

'My outlook is as wide as anybody else's,' Amos replied, hurt. 'They don't employ me on t'*Hotten Courier* because I wear blinkers!'

'Why do they, then?' wondered Henry.

Amos was trying to make a mental list of all the assets that made him a great reporter when Henry took it up again. 'All I know is that she came back from Brassington yesterday afternoon in a hired car –'

'Waste of money,' sniffed Amos.

'And she'd not have done that if she and your Mr Roper were each other's heart's desire.'

'Oh, he had to head in the other direction, happen –'

'Very devoted – takes his girl out to lunch then fails to bring her home. Nay, Amos, she was as pale as rennet curds.

55

Summat's wrong between those two – and Matt knows it.'

'I don't see as there's much he can do about it.'

'No, but there's something we can do.'

'Us?'

'Aye, Amos. Make things as easy for her as we can. Not be always on at her over every little thing.'

Henry meant 'don't *you* be on at her' but he knew better than to say so. Amos took offence even at the idea that both of them had been inconsiderate. 'I'm sure no one could have better employers,' he protested 'She gets time off whenever she wants it –'

'Then why are you always complaining when she puts in a bit of effort dressing the tree, or doing the costumes for the play?'

'That's different. That's not in her time off. She decorates the tree when she could be doing the dusting, or summat.'

'There you are. I'd rather a bit of dust than a bare Christmas tree.'

'We all have our different standards,' Amos said. 'I think cleanliness is next to Godliness.'

'I often think God must wonder about the folk who claim to be his neighbours,' Henry said.

'What?' Amos said, not understanding, but suspecting blasphemy.

'She's out now, shopping with Annie. Don't start on her the minute she comes in if she's a bit over the time.'

'Punctuality is the politeness of princes,' quoted Amos.

'My, you're a regular volume of old sayings today. There's another one – charity begins at home.'

'Humph,' said Amos.

Annie was waiting for Dolly outside the post office in Hotten. They had divided their tasks – Annie had gone to choose presents and buy charity cards, Dolly had bought a few gifts and queued for the stamps.

'There's a queue from here to next week,' she confided as she emerged. 'Now I must go and get some new decorations for the tree.'

'You don't need more, surely?'

'I haven't got any. I've been making them out of tissue paper and tin foil, but –'

'But there's a box of decorations in the cellar at t'Woolpack.'

'There never is!'

'Of course there is. They always use the same lot every year.'

'But Mr Brearley's been carrying on as if they never have a tree, and it's all my wayward idea!'

The two women smiled at each other. Annie, who had known Amos a long time, thought nothing of it. Dolly, new to the idea of a man who would put up a long and acrid defence against something he intended to have all the time, was at a loss.

They had both felt that a cup of coffee would be a life-saver and were heading towards the coffee-shop when a car drew alongside. 'Want a lift?' Richard said, putting his head out.

Dolly drew back, saying nothing. Annie took up the word. 'We've got my car, thanks.'

'How about me giving you a lift, Dolly?'

'No, thanks. I've still some shopping to do.'

'I'll wait, then.'

'No, don't!' There was panic in the tone, quickly mastered. 'I don't know how long I'll be.'

'I don't mind waiting.'

Annie didn't turn her head, but she sensed in the younger woman a fear that was rendering her helpless. She came to her rescue. 'We've things to discuss about Christmas,' she said to Richard. 'I'd like her company back in the car, Mr Roper.'

The glance he turned on her was icy. 'I *should* like to have a talk with my fiancée.'

'Later, Richard,' Dolly said, quickly. Anything to end this scene.

'This evening?'

'All right. No! – I'll be at rehearsal.'

'All evening?'

'Well . . . no . . .'

'See you at the Woolpack, then.' With a radiant smile at

Dolly and a polite little inclination of the head to Annie, he let the Citröen slide away.

'Let's have that coffee,' Annie said, thinking she looked as if she needed it.

The coffee-shop was full but they were lucky enough to get a tiny table for two near the serving hatch. The noise of orders being called drowned their conversation from anyone around, which was just as well. For Annie wanted to say something important.

'What was he doing in Hotten?' she inquired, without specifying.

Dolly's blue eyes clouded. 'Following me, I reckon.'

'Everywhere you go, he seems to be.'

She nodded. 'That seems to be his only occupation at the moment.'

'Doesn't he have anything else to do? No job?'

'No, the family has money. He ... did some fruit-growing in South Africa for a while, but he found it dull.'

'He's very handsome.'

'Oh yes.'

'And speaks well. I mean, well-mannered.'

'Yes.'

'That doesn't mean you have to marry him.'

'But ... there's more. That you don't know. Oh, it's a long, long story. I was engaged to him. I did love him.'

'Aye, well, people change over things like that, lass.'

'But he won't accept that. He claims he never changed his mind. But ... I left him, you see. I thought it would bring him to his senses. Instead, his mother made him pack up and go with her to South Africa. He says now he was so broken up by what I did that he couldn't think straight.'

'I see ...'

'But it's not true, Mrs Sugden!' Dolly said strongly. 'He just didn't have the strength to get out from under. I know it's so because later, I wrote to him.'

'After you'd left him?'

'I had a reason. I had something to tell him. Something he had to know. I thought ... if he really cares ... if there's any-

58

thing in all that talk about love ... he'll come.'

'And he didn't?'

'He didn't even reply.'

Annie could think of nothing to say. They finished their coffee. Annie said: 'Happen the letter went astray?'

'No. His mother flew over from South Africa to see me.'

'What?'

'That was his reply.'

'Oh, Dolly.'

The waitress came with the bill. Annie paid it at the cash desk while Dolly threaded her way among the tables to the door. Outside the air was cold and drizzly. The car had that strange pearly mist all over it that looks like fine cobweb. Annie unlocked, they got in and drove slowly out of the car park.

'How could his mother take on his problems like that?' Annie wondered, half to herself. She was trying to picture herself interfering between Joe and any of his friends.

'She told me she felt I'd acted with good sense. "We will consider the matter closed." I didn't know what to say. "If it's a matter of money", she said ...'

'Oh, no ...'

'Well, she never understood. You can't blame her. She felt that I probably needed money and she had plenty of that.'

They had soon left the outskirts of the little town. They were now out on the quiet country road heading towards Beckindale. Traffic was light. Annie allowed herself to turn her head for a glance at Dolly.

Tears were running down the girl's face.

'Dolly, love!' Annie cried. She brought the car to a stop on the verge and put an arm round her. 'What's the matter? What is it? Nay, don't take on like this!'

'I ... I had a baby. A little boy. He'd be two now ... I ... I had him adopted.'

'Hush, love,' Annie said, holding her close and stroking her soft hair. 'Hush, hush thee. I'm here.'

'I didn't have anybody. I didn't know what to do ... I'd written to Richard and his mother came. He didn't care about

59

the baby. "It's best to go on with the adoption," she said. I didn't know what else to do. I wanted to keep him but I didn't see how I could get a job and look after him ...'

'No, I know, it's difficult. What about your own family, your mother?'

'Oh!' Dolly shook her head, burrowing further into Annie's shoulder. 'She wouldn't even speak to me.'

'Dear girl, poor lass, there, there,' soothed Annie. 'It's in the past.'

'But my baby's gone, hasn't he? To a good home, I know that. I've never seen him since. Mrs Roper offered me money to ensure I went on with the adoption but I wouldn't take it. I tore up the cheque and threw it in her face.'

'Good for thee,' Annie said.

'Now Richard's back. He says he didn't know what was going on. I know it's not true. He let her take over because he couldn't face it. Now she's dead – a boating accident last year. Now he feels alone, lonely. Now he wants his wife, he wants his son. But ... but ...'

'Lass, you don't need to fear him. He can't blackmail you.'

'But you don't understand. He's got money. He can hire detectives. That's how he found me at the Woolpack. He'll find out where the baby is and try to get him back.'

'Nay, love, he wouldn't do that.'

'You don't know him!'

'That's true,' Annie said, gently smoothing the hair away from her forehead as Dolly sat up to look at her in despair. 'But I know you, and I think you'll talk him out of it.'

'I don't know how. He doesn't even *listen*.'

For a while they sat silent. Then Dolly said, 'Don't tell Matt!'

'Of course not, Dolly.'

'I wouldn't ever want him to know.'

Annie shook her head. 'He would understand.'

'No! No, it's bad enough to live with a man, and have his child – but to give the child away!' Dolly's voice broke. 'When he speaks about his children, I hear it in Matt's voice. They meant the world to him. He wouldn't understand a girl who gives her baby away.'

'You underestimate him,' Annie murmured. 'And one day you'll see that, and you'll tell him all this yourself.'

'No! I couldn't bear it! I've come to the conclusion the only thing to do is leave Beckindale.'

'Don't say that, Dolly. Don't run away.'

'I don't see what else to do. I'm only causing embarrassment to everybody.'

'We can bear a bit of embarrassment, my dear. We're not likely to melt in the rain, like sugar dollies.'

Unexpectedly Dolly smiled. It was like the sun coming out through rain. 'I wish I'd had someone like you to help me years ago,' she sighed. 'I've a feeling you could even cope with Richard.'

Richard had driven away from his encounter with them in a furious temper at not being able to wheedle Dolly to accompany him. He had masked his anger with the good manners he had learned as a boy – he often used them as a defence and a weapon. He couldn't understand why in this setting, they seemed to win him no friends. He'd always come out on top in other situations.

After driving around aimlessly for an hour or so, he headed towards Beckindale. On the Cross Field Road, he espied a man at the side bending over something.

No need to examine that figure more closely. Richard knew at once it was Matt Skilbeck. For one mad moment he was tempted to slam his foot down and run him down. But that would gain him nothing. He slowed to a stop, to find Matt was talking gently to a sheep lying on the verge.

'What's up?'

'Hit and run, I reckon,' Matt said, turning his head. There was no way anyone could have told, by his manner, that he had felt a chill when he heard that voice.

'And they didn't stop?'

'They seldom do. I think they don't realise that beasts can suffer. There, old girl, keep still. I'll fetch t'Land-Rover for thee.'

'Can I help?' Richard said, the well-mannered public schoolboy.

'Well ... happen you could fetch Joe? You know Joe?'

61

'I've seen him around.'

'He'll be by the biggest barn, loading drainage pipes. The farm's down this road, left at t'fork –'

'I know where it is,' Richard said.

'Tell him I'm up by Cross Lane End.'

'Okay.' Richard made as if to move off, then said, 'Could we have a chat? Not now – when you're not busy.'

'I'm always around.'

'But you're always busy.'

Matt hesitated. 'This is a busy time for us. Christmas, the Nativity Play, lambing to get ready for, drainage gone wrong at Clicker Bottom ...'

'It's about Dolly.'

Matt met his eyes. 'I thought it were.'

Richard expected to outface him. They looked at one another. It was Richard who let his gaze fall. 'I'd better go and get Joe,' he said.

Matt, kneeling by the injured ewe after he'd gone, let himself speculate about Richard for a moment. What kind of a man was that? He must see he was making Dolly unhappy. It was no use arriving and saying he had a claim on her from way back – claims were no use unless the other party acknowledged them, and Dolly clearly didn't agree that they had any bond between them.

But he was so persistent. You could see him wearing Dolly down, fraying her nerves, so that in the end she might just give in to have some peace.

He mustn't let that happen. But ... how could he prevent it? He had no rights over her. He liked her, she liked him, but that was as far as it went. At least, that was as far as it went on Dolly's side. For himself, he was beginning to feel that life without her would be hard to face. The feeling had grown more and more insistent as Richard Roper harassed her and seemed likely to take her away.

If Dolly would just say: 'Help me, Matt!' If she would make some sign ... Why didn't she? Why didn't she call on their friendship?

The only reason must be that this was too delicate a matter

to call in some blundering outsider. And that being so, Matt knew where he stood. She felt he was a friend, but not a close enough friend to turn to in a personal crisis.

Sighing, he soothed the sheep. 'Quiet, now, lass,' he said. 'There's no sense making things worse ... We're all too ready to do that.'

Richard reached the farm in five minutes and sent Joe off on his mission. But instead of turning about and driving away, Richard went to the door of the farm and knocked.

The woman who had been with Dolly in Hotten opened to his knock. There was something about her that impressed him. He had the feeling that if he could get her on his side, he'd be able to persuade Dolly.

'May I come in?' he asked.

She looked taken aback. Then she stood aside in welcome. Few people had ever been refused a welcome at Emmerdale.

'I've just sent Joe ... your son, is it? ... to help Matt with an injured sheep.'

'That was good of you. Come in, sit thee down. I'm getting dinner, but can I offer you anything? Tea? Coffee?'

Richard would have said yes to a stiff scotch, but he could tell this wasn't the kind of home where they offered such things. 'No, thanks,' he said. 'I ... would just like a few words with you. About Dolly and your son.'

'Dolly and Joe?'

'No, Matt.'

'Ah.' She looked into the saucepan simmering on the stove. 'Matt is my son-in-law.'

'He's married?' That staggered him.

'He's a widower. My daughter Peggy died three years ago.'

'I see. Yet he stays on here?'

'This is his home.'

He was silent. The quiet conviction of the words, the almost offhand way she busied herself with the preparations for the meal while speaking to him, seemed to cut him down to size.

'I asked Matt to meet so we could have a talk. I don't know when it's ever going to happen. He's so ... taken up with things.'

'We've a farm to run here, Mr Roper. There's really only Joe and Matt. My father helps, but he's getting on. Happen you've never seen moorland farmers at work before. You have to keep at it.'

She was now setting places at the table. 'Does Dolly come in to lunch?' he asked, suddenly scared she'd come in and find him there. He felt alien, out of key.

'No, she's opening up at the Woolpack now. She has a snack with Amos and Henry when it's quiet.'

'It's ... it's not really the life for her.'

'She seems to like it.'

'No!' Then the anger in the word struck him, and he tried to amend it. 'It's not what I want for my wife-to-be.'

Annie turned to look full at him. She put down the cutlery she was holding. 'But is she to be your wife, Mr Roper? That's the question.'

'I love her,' he said.

She took a moment before replying. 'Dolly is an easy girl to love. We're all fond of Dolly.'

'I'm not just "fond". I *love* her. I'm going to marry her.'

'That's up to Dolly.'

'It would all be so easy if you weren't all against me!'

Annie studied his handsome, petulant face. Why, he's a child, she thought. 'We're not against you,' she said. 'We don't know you.'

'But you've changed Dolly. She used to be ... I don't know ... She and I understood each other.'

'That's as may be. But time's gone by since then, and Dolly's not the same person any more.'

'She has to be!' He burst out. 'I need her! And there's more – that you don't know about.'

'Mr Roper, I don't need to know everything to be sure that you're making that lass unhappy. You only have to look at her. Since you came into the district, she's like a ghost. Why don't you just leave her alone?'

'I can't. You don't understand. Everything that would give my life meaning is with Dolly.'

'That's not so. I've been through trouble, Mr Roper – and

64

believe me, so has Matt – and life can be renewed. It takes time and determination, but it can be done.'

'That's what it's taking in my case,' he said, with a faint attempt at a joke. 'Time – it's taken me months to track her down. And determination. I'm determined to have her back.'

'Track her down? You speak as if she were a creature you were hunting –'

'The ends justified the means! You don't know! I had to find her and make her marry me – because that's the only way I can have my son.'

He watched her as he hurled this at her, expecting shock and disapproval to show in her eyes. Annie disappointed him. She put her hands on the back of a chair and leaned on it. 'Where were you when the baby was born?' she inquired.

He was startled. 'You knew?'

'Tell me where you were, Mr Roper. When your son came into the world.'

'I ... I wasn't there. I admit it ... But it wasn't my fault. There were family pressures –'

'So strong that you were prevented standing by the mother of your own child?'

'You don't understand. My mother ... she was in touch with Dolly. She ... She said there was a doubt it actually was my child.'

'Mr Roper!' Anne stiffened, and without actually taking a step seemed to draw away from him.

'Oh, I know – I was a fool – I knew it wasn't true, really. I knew she wasn't that kind of girl. But my mother ... You have to live with a woman like that to know what strength she has. She'd always been able to make me do what she wanted. I defied her at first over Dolly but ... well ... she won, in the end. I'm not defending myself. I'm here now to try to make things right again.'

Annie shook her head a little. 'You know what you remind me of? You're like a boy that's going to watch a procession. But something else that seems more important takes up your attention and when you get to the place – the parade's gone by. Don't you understand, Mr Roper? The parade's gone by, the band has played its last tune, the music has died away. You weren't there.'

'But these things aren't just once and never more! Dolly loved me, she really did. And I loved her, and still do. It can be like it was.'

'No it can't. Dolly was a carefree girl when you first took up with her. She's had a baby, had to give it up.'

'But we can get the baby back,' he said eagerly. 'I've got detectives —'

'I'm no expert in these things, but I gather the lad's been legally adopted. You couldn't get him back if you had all the detectives of Scotland Yard.'

'But I could give him a good life! I've got money —'

'You should have said all this two years ago.'

'I'm saying it now! I want my son! I have a right to him, haven't I? I wasn't consulted about the home he had to go to —'

'Why should anyone consult you? You weren't there, and you weren't Dolly's husband.' Annie let go of the chair on which she'd been leaning and came to his side. She put a hand on his shoulder. 'Mr Roper, think what you're doing. Dolly's a grown woman. You can't force her to do owt she doesn't want to do. If you talked her into marrying you, well ... you'd both regret it, and you know it.'

'What you're telling me is that you want me out of the way so that your son-in-law can have a clear field.'

Annie took her hand away as if she had been stung. 'I'm not a schemer, Mr Roper. Don't judge others by yourself.'

He jerked his head up. 'That's the first unkind thing you've said to me. You've said your say, but you haven't shown dislike.'

'I don't dislike you. I just don't understand you. You come here, seized by some whim to find the girl you didn't bother about three years ago when she wrote to say she was pregnant, and who was offered money by your mother when time came to have the baby adopted. I don't understand folk like that.'

'It's easy enough,' he said, his tone weary. 'I'm lonely.'

'Aye? Now your mother's gone, there's no one to direct your life, is that it? Well, don't come asking Dolly to take it on. Dolly doesn't want you.'

'You don't know that!'

'I do indeed. She told me so. And since she doesn't welcome you here, neither do I. I've heard you out and I see she's right. So I'd be glad if you'd leave, Mr Roper.'

Even he, stranger to the district, knew how enormous this step was. Annie Sugden had almost never shown anyone the door in her life.

He rose to his feet. He was taller than she by about four inches. He stared down at her. 'You're strong,' he said. 'But so am I. And no one can prevent me from finding my son. Tell Dolly.'

'I'll carry no such message.'

'It doesn't matter. I'll tell her this evening. I'm seeing her then. She'll know – she'll understand.'

'She understands already, I assure you. And I'll tell you this – you'll never get a lass like Dolly Acaster to tell you owt that would harm the happiness of a child.'

He frowned. 'You think a lot of her, don't you?'

'I care about the lass.'

'Then take heed. I can make her very unhappy.'

'Save your breath, lad,' Annie said. 'And now if you don't mind, I'm busy. I've a meal to serve.'

When the door had closed on him, Annie picked up the handful of cutlery she'd been placing, and resumed her work. But then suddenly she began to tremble. The knives and forks spilled on to the table. She sank down on a chair.

'Ah, lass, lass,' she murmured, 'what are we going to do?'

CHAPTER FIVE

Joe and Matt came in for the midday meal looking depressed. The sheep had died despite all their efforts. Sam expressed sympathy, but his main subject of conversation was the Butterworth Ball.

'I can't understand it,' he said. 'Nobody from Robblesfield's been in –'

'Yes, they have. I saw Bert Hover and his lad in the bar the other night,' Joe said.

'What I was going to say was, "Nobody from Robblesfield's been in that seems to have any interest in t'Ball",' Sam continued with a glance of reproach at his grandson. 'I don't understand why they took it if they're not going to make a fuss about it.'

'Happen they didn't take it after all, Grandad,' Matt suggested.

'Huh! And happen Christmas won't come on December 25th! They've got it. I know they have. I feel it in my bones.'

'Are you finished with the stew or shall I take it away?' his daughter put in.

'I'll have a drop more, lass. Nobody makes leek and lamb stew like thee.'

'How's the play going?' Joe asked.

Matt shook his head. 'It's at a standstill. Nobody seems to understand what it's on about. I mean, we all know it's the story of the Nativity, but we don't know what the characters are saying. I wish Mr Hinton hadn't decided to use such a funny version.'

'Dolly were saying you're coming on with your lines.'

'Aye,' Matt said, but said no more.

He went out soon after, while the others were still eating their pudding. Sam said: 'He's upset. You can see that.'

'That feller Roper's some opposition,' Joe said.

'I don't see that! You couldn't ask for a finer man than Matt,' Sam said fiercely.

'I know—I'm on your side, Grandad. But the other lad's ruthless. Matt won't fight dirty.'

'Trouble is,' Sam said with a sigh, 'Matt's so gentle and humble it doesn't dawn on him that Dolly could love him.'

'And you think she does?' Joe said, startled. His grandfather rarely came out in such strong terms about personal matters.

'Well, of course, I'm old and it's a long time since I had to think about things like that. But I still recognise that look in a girl's eyes – and it's there when Dolly looks at Matt.'

'But you wouldn't want Matt to get married, Grandad.'

Sam put his spoon and fork together on his pudding plate and pushed it away. 'I could live with it,' he said. 'Specially when it's Dolly. A rare idea of hers, that about putting a replica up in the niche. Saved our faces.'

There was a tap on the outer door. Annie tensed. She feared it might be Richard back again. But she found Lesley Gibson on the doorstep when she opened. 'Come in, come in,' she said.

'Am I being a nuisance? Are you still having lunch?'

'Nay, we generally eat early. Can I offer you something?'

'No, thanks,' Lesley said, though she eyed the remains of the Wilfra apple pie with longing. 'I'm needed back home. We've had a fuse.' She looked expectantly at Joe.

He said, 'Can't mend a fuse? So much for women's lib.'

'Smartypants, I can mend a fuse – but not without fuse wire. I've come a-borrowing.'

'I'll get thee some,' Sam said, rising. He wasn't sure he approved of Lesley. Girls who knew too much about brewing and used expressions like 'smartypants' were not his type.

He went out to his shed. He knew just where to lay hands on fuse wire. When he came back, Lesley and Joe were talking about some encounter they'd had at the Bear and Staff.

'But his girlfriend's quite nice,' Lesley was saying. 'I happened on her in Connelton this morning, and she's con-

69

versible enough when he's not there butting in.'

'Whose girlfriend?' Sam inquired.

'Little Teaker.'

'Oh, him,' Sam said. 'Drinks more than his brother sells.'

'I think Lily has just about had enough of that problem. I gathered they'd had a tiff. She said he'd pushed off to London.'

'London must be fun at this time of year,' Joe said with envy.

'No it isn't, it's full of traffic and the shops are awful, with Christmas shoppers piling in. Hey, by the way – talking of Christmas – would you like a new cricket ball for Christmas, Joe?'

An extraordinary pause ensued. Joe stared at her, Sam sank down on the nearest chair.

'What's the matter?' Lesley said. 'What have I said?'

'What ever made you think of buying a cricket ball?' Sam managed to ask.

'Is it something women shouldn't offer to buy? Have I barged into some male chauvinist pig stronghold?'

'What put it into your head, Lesley?' Joe insisted.

'Well ... Lily did.'

'Her that we met at the Bear and Staff?'

'With Little Teaker?' Sam said in a squeak of horror.

'Yes, the same. Why? What's wrong?'

'What's wrong? Little Teaker is only younger brother to Fred Teaker, licensee of the Miller's Arms in Robblesfield that's all.'

'I'm sorry?' Lesley said, her eyebrows up. 'I don't follow Mr Pearson.'

'Never mind, never mind. Lily – Little's girlfriend – she talked to you about cricket balls?'

Lesley looked as if she was stifling a very bawdy comment. 'All she said was, "Doing Christmas shopping? I hear you could be a pal to your boyfriend's mates by buying him a cricket ball."'

'There!' groaned Sam. 'Who else could she have heard that from but Little Teaker?'

'Now, now, Dad, don't get in a state,' Annie warned.

'What's the matter? Have I said something awful? I wish I understood –'

'Aye! *I* understand, lass. That's what matters. Little Teaker. Why didn't we think of it? He was there one night in the bar.'

'I even think it was that very night, Grandad. And he drinks like a fish –'

'And the whisky was gone.'

'And everyone lived happily ever after,' Lesley said, mystified. 'What are we on about?'

'The less you know, the better, Miss Gibson. Just you forget it. We've troubles enough.'

Lesley looked at Joe, and was relieved to see he didn't seem to think the Day of Judgement was about to descend on them. 'Come on, I'll walk you part way home.'

'Oh, you really are gallant,' she teased, and went out with him.

'I must go at once and warn Amos,' Sam began.

'No, you don't, Dad. You're all upset and you've been working in the vegetables all morning and you should have a nap –'

'I must speak to Amos –'

'Then ring him up.'

'I couldn't talk on the telephone about something as important as this, Annie!' her father cried, shocked at the mere idea. His experience from speaking with Jack in Rome was that operators kept butting in.

'All right then, go and see him if you must – but not until you've had a rest. You'll make yourself poorly again.'

There were times when Sam knew he had the upper hand and there were times when he heard the voice of authority. He was moreover physically very tired from a morning's digging in preparation of a new celery trench. He submitted.

When Dolly came home for her afternoon break she found the house quiet. Sam was asleep upstairs, Annie had gone out to talk to Mr Hinton about whether anything else needed to be done to the vicarage garden while they had the scout troop available to help. Joe and Matt were still struggling with the big pool of water that had inexplicably collected at Clicker End. She came into the warm kitchen and after taking off her coat and scooter helmet, put on the kettle for a cup of tea. While it boiled she warmed her hands at a distance from the kettle's sides.

She heard Matt's footsteps before he entered. She braced herself. He came in looking tired and mud-stained. 'Hello,' he said. 'Making tea?'

'Aye.'

'I'll take us a flask back. It's cold dirty work down there.'

'How's it going?'

'Blessed thing's a mystery. Joe's Dad must've put the pipes in at too high a level. Certainly can't find 'em where the water's collecting.'

He washed his hands then went searching in the dresser drawer for some paper and a pencil. 'We need to make a sketch,' he explained.

'Aye.' She poured tea for herself and Matt, then put the rest in a flask. 'Richard told me about the sheep,' she said. 'How is it?'

'It died.'

'Oh.' Tears came flooding into her eyes.

Matt came close to her. 'Dolly, lass, what is it? Why are you so moithered by him?'

'It's all in the past ...'

'He asked if he could speak to me. I think he's going to be around this evening, from the way he spoke.'

She made up her mind suddenly. 'I'd rather you heard it from me than from him, Matt,' she said. 'Perhaps if you hear it from me, it won't sound so bad.'

'How could it be bad?' he objected. 'Not about you, Dolly.'

'Oh, why do you have to think good of everybody?' she cried wildly. 'You don't know! I did a terrible thing. I lived with Richard. We were engaged.'

Matt's face went quiet. He said nothing. His eyes were fastened on Dolly's.

'We broke up – it was my doing, I wanted to force him to

72

a decision. His mother didn't approve, she took him abroad. She thought I was beneath him.'

'Nay –'

'Let me finish, Matt. After he'd gone away I found I was pregnant. I let him know, but he didn't do anything so I had the baby adopted.' Tears were spilling down over her cheeks. Only the last remnants of strength kept her there, facing him.

'He let his baby be adopted?'

'His mother thought it was best. Now she's dead and he wants things back the way they were.'

'That's why you're so afraid of him?'

'I've reason to be, Matt. You don't know. Money can do a lot of harm.'

'Dolly –'

'I'm going away. I've got to get away.'

'With him?'

'Never!' she blurted. 'No matter what he says.'

'Then why are you going? Don't go, Dolly.'

He saw her courage crumble. 'Some things get spoilt, Matt. The past casts a shadow, drains away the sunlight.'

'But where'll you go?'

'Home. My mother's had an asthma attack, feels the need of company for Christmas –'

'But you don't get on with her –'

'Oh, Matt!' she cried, as she turned to run. 'Anywhere's better than here!'

Her words struck him to stone. Unhappiness had spoiled everything to such an extent that she couldn't bear Emmerdale any more. He hesitated, about to go upstairs after her, but with a shake of the head he turned away. What was the use? All he could do was tell her what she surely knew – that Emmerdale was home if she wanted it to be, that they would keep her safe from anyone who tried to harm her.

He had to get back to Joe at Clicker End. He even remembered to take the flask of hot tea.

When Sam woke, his daughter was home from her afternoon visit. He could smell an inviting aroma of toasted muffin.

73

He got up, stretched, put on his slippers, dashed some cold water on his face to rouse himself, and went downstairs.

'Soon's I've had afternoon tea, I'm going to t'Woolpack –'

'Not in this?' Annie objected, nodding at the window.

Rain was teeming down outside. 'Eeh,' Sam said. 'I didn't know it had come on stair rods.'

'Why don't you just ring Amos?'

'I told you, it's too delicate.'

'You don't have to say much. Just enough to put him on his guard,' she suggested.

Sam thought about it. There was no doubt, he was as capable of diplomacy as anyone else. He went to the phone, dialled the Woolpack, and when Amos replied he roared: 'Is that you, Amos?'

Amos held the phone away from his ear. 'Of course it's me, Mr Pearson.'

'Amos, I want to speak to you about a certain item.'

'About what?' Sam was shouting so loud that the microphone vibrated and it was almost impossible to understand what he was saying.

'About our pride and joy. *You* know.'

'About –? Oh, aye. What, Mr Pearson?'

'Certain information has come into my possession –'

'Certain what?'

'*Information!*' bellowed Sam. 'About that item.'

'Information about the, I mean, about that ornament?'

'Aye, that's it. There's great danger, Amos. *Danger!*'

'Danger?' moaned Amos.

'A crisis may be approaching. I intend to take action.'

'You what?'

'*Action!*'

'Oh, aye. I see. Yes, well, all right. But what can I do?'

'Ward off all inquiries –'

'Ward of what?'

'Oh, never mind!' cried Sam. 'I'll come and talk to you when rain stops!'

As Amos put the phone down, Henry Wilks joined him. 'What was that about?' he asked. 'I could hear Sam roaring from t'back room.'

'He says there's danger, Mr Wilks.' Amos suddenly heard the word. 'Danger!'

'What kind of danger?'

'I don't know! He didn't make that clear. But it's to t'ball, I know it is!'

Henry looked unconvinced. 'Danger? What kind of danger could there be?'

Amos pondered. 'One thing's sure. We ought to take precautions. I daren't think how it would look if anything happened to t'ball.'

'But that isn't t'ball, Amos.'

'That's the point! Don't you see?' he exclaimed. 'Looked at from t'other side of t'bar, that ball looks like t'Butterworth Ball. But if anybody were actually to get to it and pick it up, they'd soon know the difference. Anybody's who's handled the real one would see that this one was made more recent, and by a different maker.'

Even Henry had to admit there was truth in that. 'But who's going to pick this one up?' he asked.

'Nobody, if I can help it!' retorted Amos.

He hurried off. He had just the thing. Somewhere in the attic he had an old electric bell and an adaptor. With that, he would rig up an alarm.

He came downstairs again with the dust-covered contraption. It took him quite a time to clean it sufficiently to find the screws and undo it. Then, with batteries, he tested it. By minute adjustments he managed matters so that a little metal plate would react to a release of pressure: while a weight rested on its surface, the bell remained silent. When the weight was picked up, the bell rang.

Henry watched this performance with interest. 'Where are you going to put the actual bell?' he inquired.

'Here in t'back room.'

'What if somebody creeps in in the night? Would you hear the bell from upstairs?'

'I'll ... er ... amplify it at night.'

'Amplify it? You're never going to buy an amplifier?'

75

Amos got up from the kitchen table, fetched a tin plate, set the bell on it, picked up the weight off the metal surface, and the bell rang like the last trump. The tin plate actually danced in vibration.

'Bye,' said Henry, 'I don't think you'd sleep through that!'

Problems began when Amos took the device out to the bar. First of all, the wire wasn't long enough. That involved him in another scramble in the attic to find some extra bell wire. He joined the new wire to the old. He got a prick in his finger. 'Ouch,' he said.

'Need any help?' asked Henry.

'Certainly not. I'm ex-Artillery, you know.'

'But this is a bell, Amos, not a fourteen-pounder.'

'Just stand aside, Mr Wilks, if you please and we'll see how well it works.'

He tacked the wire to the skirting board behind the bar and out to the back room. He disguised its emergence from the niche with a Christmas streamer. He put the ball on the little metal plate. He went into the back room and switched on at the wall socket.

'Now,' he said to Henry. 'Pick it up.'

Obediently Henry picked up the ball.

Nothing.

'Shouldn't it ring?' Henry asked.

'Oh, heck,' said Amos, and hurried back to the wall socket. He tested all the connections, checked the wiring, switched off and on a couple of times.

The bell rang under his hand, nearly scaring him out of his socks.

He dashed out to the bar. 'Did you pick up the ball?' he demanded.

'No, I just put it down,' said Henry.

The ball was sitting in its niche, round and serene, and the bell was ringing fit to burst in the back room. 'I thought it was supposed to ring when it was picked up?' Henry said.

'There's a fault.'

'Happen you've wired it up in reverse?'

'You can't reverse the wiring. The wiring's got to go into

those connections. When t'ball's on t'plate, the weight keeps the connection switched off. When t'ball's picked up, the connection clicks together.'

'Have you read the instructions?'

'There aren't any instructions. This is an ordinary door bell. I've adapted it.'

'Well, couldn't you arrange it so that the metal plate drops down when the ball is picked up?'

'How can you keep a two inch metal plate up in the air, Mr Wilks? By interfering with the laws of gravity?'

'We-ell,' Henry said doubtfully, 'couldn't it go like this?' He tipped the little metal plate up so that it was on its edge, set the ball in front of it. He picked up the ball and the little plate fell forward into place.

Amos stared at it. 'That . . . might work,' he agreed.

He rushed away to the wall switch and switched off while he made the adjustment. Then he put the plate up on edge, set the ball in position, eyed the whole thing, and returned to the switch.

He switched on. The sound of the bell rang out from the bar. Amos flew back there. 'Did you pick up the ball?'

'Nay,' said Henry, gaping at it. The ball was safely in its niche. The bell went on ringing. Amos picked it up. The racket stopped.

'I could have told you that wouldn't work,' Amos said. 'I do have some experience with things like this, y'know.'

'Seems to me,' Henry said, 'you can have an alarm that tells you when the ball's safe but not when it's being pinched.'

'Just you leave it to me, Mr Wilks. I'll sort it. I've come to the conclusion that something's wrong with the adaptor.'

' "Then do not send to know for whom the bell tolls," Henry quoted, "it tolls for thee." '

'Pardon?'

'Nothing, Amos.'

All Amos's efforts to make the alarm system work were unavailing. The principles were clear, the wiring was correct, the switch at the wall worked with everything he tried as a test. But the bell wouldn't work.

Opening time was near. He dismantled his contraption and stowed it away. He tidied himself up, let Dolly in, got some mixers up from the cellar, and made sure the till was cashed up. Then he opened the door to Walter.

Walter was the only customer for a while, but that was quite usual. Amos didn't know it, but Sam was even then on his way to the Woolpack, the rain having eased up a little.

But before Sam could appear, an unexpected visitor came in. Fred Teaker, licensee of the Miller's Arms in Robblesfield, turned up ordering a pint.

Amos was aghast. It took all his will power not to turn his head to eye the supposed Butterworth Ball. 'How do,' said Fred.

'How do you do, Mr Teaker. I think you'll enjoy that,' Amos said, setting the ale before him.

'On the house, is this?' Fred inquired, quaffing it.

Amos was about to retort that his method was cash only. But he thought better of it. 'Be my guest,' he said. 'A fellow licencee, after all.'

'Ah,' said Fred. He turned and leaned back against the bar. 'Not making a fortune here, are you?'

'Trade's always slow first thing. My clients like to go home and tidy up before they drop in.'

'Oh? Too posh to have working men?'

'Nowt o't'sort,' Amos said. 'It's just that there's an appreciation of my efforts to give them a pleasant environment, like.'

'Hm.' Fred drank more ale, then turned to put his glass on the counter. 'Come to see the Butterworth Ball, do they?' he asked, nodding towards the niche.

Amos preferred to avoid a direct reply. 'This is the centre of village activity,' he said. 'Of course you've competition in Robblesfield, haven't you? Ring o' Bells.'

'Ring o' Bells is no more worry to me than Malt Shovel is to you,' Fred said, feeling about for his pipe. 'Had that display shelf made special for it, did you?'

'You could say so,' Amos said. He had no objection to agreeing to that. The shelf was genuine.

'We can't offer it a home like that,' Fred said.

'Pardon?'

'When it comes to us.'

'Oh ... Next season, you mean. But you've got to win it first.'

'Oh, earlier than that, I hope.'

'I ... er ... don't see quite ...'

'We want to take it off you.'

'Eh?'

'Y'see, Mr Brearley, this is the two hundredth anniversary of the granting of the licence to the Miller's Arms in Robblesfield. Granted at the sessions just before Christmas, it was. I been thinking ...'

'What?' Amos asked with trembling lips.

'That nothing could make a better contribution to the celebration than the Butterworth Ball, in a place of honour in the Miller's Arms.'

CHAPTER SIX

To say that Amos was in a state of panic would be the understatement of the century.

'I ... er ... The third week of December?'

'That's the bi-centenary date.' Fred looked pleased with himself. 'Bi-centenary,' he repeated, savouring it. 'This place ain't two hundred years old ...'

'Er ... no ...'

'It only looks it! Haw-haw!' And Fred went off into a peal of laughter.

His mirth gave Amos a chance to recover. 'I'd have to direct you to Sam Pearson about borrowing t'ball,' he said. 'He's chairman of cricket team.'

'Borrowing?' Fred bridled. 'You don't own it, tha knows! You've only got tenure of it.' He gazed at the ball. 'Looks as if it could do with a bit of a clean up.' Now he leaned forward over the counter, bringing his head at least twelve inches nearer the ball. 'I don't remember it being that mucky when we parted with it.'

'Mucky?' Amos echoed, greatly affronted. 'Let me tell you, nowt in this inn is mucky –'

'Just hand it me a sec, will you, lass?' Fred said suddenly to Dolly, who had been serving others at the far end of the bar.

Thus called to action, Dolly turned. 'Hand what?'

'That there ball.'

Dolly raised her hand.

'No!' exclaimed Amos.

'Eh?' Fred said.

'Can't take it off,' Amos said, his brain working with the unexpected speed of lightning. 'It's been wired.'

'Wired?'

'Take it off, a bell starts ringing.'

'You what?' scoffed Fred.

'It's a burglar alarm.'

Fred looked at him with his bushy eyebrows raised. 'Fitted up a burglar alarm? You've had reason to be afraid o' burglars?'

'Not at all, not at all,' Amos said. 'But ... I take my responsibilities seriously.'

'Pick it up, then. Let's hear it ring.'

'I ... er ... don't feel I've the right to handle it.'

'But you must've handled it when you had the alarm set up?'

'No ... yes ... I ...'

'Pick it up.' Fred was clearly determined. 'I want to hear it ring. Might try it out in my place, for some of the silver cups we win at darts.'

In despair, Amos put out a trembling hand and let it hover over the ball. He knew the bell wouldn't ring. He would say there was a short-circuit.

He picked up the ball.

The bell rang.

' 'Bye!' cried Fred. 'That's clever! No fear of it ever being stolen, is there?'

Amos stared at the ball as if it were bewitched. Slowly, with apprehension, he put it back. The bell stopped ringing.

With a tremendous effort he turned back to Fred, his face composed. 'You see we take it serious,' he said. 'Can't say yes or no about lending it to you for the centenary –'

'Bi-centenary.'

'Bi-centenary. That lies with Mr Pearson. He's chairman of the organising committee for cricket season.'

'Be no trouble there, will there. We only want to borrow it for a couple o' weeks.'

'You'll have to see Sam. I do nowt wi'out him saying so.'

Fred gave Amos a very hard stare. 'All right then. I'll see him. I'll pop up to Emmerdale and have a word.'

He finished his ale in a gulp, nodded all round, and left.

Amos leaned on the counter, his heart thumping. Never, in all his many escapades as a reporter for the *Hotten Courier*, had he been in a situation more fraught with danger. After a moment he turned to Dolly.

'It worked,' he whispered.

'Well, you wanted it to.'

'But it wasn't wired up!'

'What?' Dolly said, astounded.

'It ... it's divine intervention.'

'Rubbish,' said Henry Wilks, coming in from the back room. 'I'll have a whisky, Amos. On the house. I've just saved your bacon.'

'*You* have, Mr Wilks?'

'Who do you think was ringing bells for you?'

'You?'

'Me.'

'But ... but ... how did you know when to ring, and to stop?'

'Amos, Amos,' sighed Henry. 'Why do we have a mirror hanging on that wall so that we can see it from t'back room? It's so we can see if anybody's come into t'bar and is waiting to be served while we're taking a break. Eh?'

'Oh ... aye.'

81

'So I watched in t'mirror. And when you picked up t'ball, I joined the ends of the wires, and when you put it back I took 'em apart.'

'You ... But ... how did you know Fred was there? How did you know what to do? You were out –'

'I came in t'back door about halfway through your conversation wi' him. He was talking loud enough, by heaven. Wanted all the world to know he was asking to borrow the ball.'

'Mr Wilks!' Amos said. He mopped his brow. 'I must say ... though I don't approve of deceit ...'

'Oh no. That's why we've got a replacement ball in that niche –'

'I don't *approve*. Never have. But I must say, you've done a helpful thing this night.'

Henry looked at Amos. 'Be careful, Amos. You'll actually say something complimentary if you're not careful.'

'Not but what,' his partner went on, 'it's only what you ought to have done, because your reputation as partner in this business is just as much at stake as mine, if the theft of the ball is ever discovered.'

Henry grinned. 'I spoke too soon. Well, what about that whisky?'

'What whisky?'

'The one I earned for coming to your rescue.'

'Oh,' said Amos. 'But we've just said, haven't we, that it was your duty to do it. Nobody should get special treats for doing their duty.'

'You mean I'm going to have to pay for it myself?' But he'd expected that all along. He seldom won a round with Amos.

He was taking his first sip when Sam came galloping in. 'Amos, Amos –'

'Sam!' Amos came from behind the bar to meet him. 'You've seen Fred Teaker? Oh, don't say you said owt to him –'

'Fred Teaker? Nay, it's about Little Teaker –'

'Little Teaker? No, no, it was Fred –'

82

'Will you listen to me, Amos? I tell you, it was Little –'

Dolly came up. 'Sit thee down, Mr Pearson. I'll get thee a drink. What'll it be?'

'Eh ... cider, thanks, lass. I will sit down. I don't mind admitting, my knees are all ashake.'

'How didsta know he was coming in?' Amos asked.

'Who? Little?'

'Nay, Fred.'

'But I'm talking about Little!'

Henry said: 'Could I make a suggestion? Suppose you each say what you have to say from t'beginning without interrupting each other.'

Sam glowered at him, but accepted his cider with thankfulness. Since he wanted to swallow some, Amos was able to get in first with his story, which was just as well, as he was bursting to tell it.

Sam listened with growing consternation. 'He knows,' he groaned.

'Knows what?'

'That that –' he nodded towards the niche – 'that's not t'real ball.'

'How can he know? He said it were a bit more mucky, but he couldn't possibly –'

'He knows, Amos,' Sam repeated, and told them what he had heard from Lesley Gibson at midday.

Amos and Sam were in a state of gloom. Even Henry wasn't without some dismay. It wouldn't sound too good over the surrounding district if a story of jiggery-pokery got out. At the very least they'd be the laughing stock of the dales. At worst, they could lose custom.

'What are we going to do?' muttered Amos.

'One thing's certain. We're not going to lend that ball to Fred Teaker.'

'I'm with you there.'

'What I don't understand,' Henry remarked, 'is why he came here asking for the ball. He's got the real one – why didn't he just put it on display, let anybody handle it that wanted to so's to verify it was the real one, and leave us to cope with the rush of angry questions that'd follow?'

'Wants to cause us as much misery as he can,' said Sam.

'Oh, come on, Sam —'

'You don't know them Robblesfield lot. He wants us to suffer.'

'I dunno,' murmured Henry. 'Mebbe his mind works different from mine, but if I'd had the Butterworth Ball and wanted to chalk one up against Beckindale, I'd have gone about it different.'

'He's doing us all the damage he can.'

'Nay, he isn't. He's almost given us warning. You know what I think?'

'What?'

'Fred Teaker knows t'Butterworth Ball is missing — but *he* hasn't got it.'

'Yes he has. His brother took it.'

'Aye. So what? Little Teaker took it — that's almost sure. But there's no proof he'd give it to Fred. Don't I gather there's no love lost between them?'

'That's true,' said Amos, nodding with vehemence.

'You think Little's still got it, then?'

'I dunno, Sam. Doesn't do us much good if he has. He's gone to London, you just said.'

'Oh, Lord help us,' sighed Sam with unpretended piety.

For the moment there was nothing to be done, except wait. With concealed misery, Amos went back to cope with the influx of evening customers.

Richard Roper came in about a quarter past eight. He'd had an excellent dinner at the Red Lion in Brassington, but had felt impelled to drive fast to get to Beckindale and the lesser elegance of the Woolpack.

Dolly was busy. Richard bought himself a drink from Amos then took it to a table at the far side. Joe Sugden was sitting there, obviously waiting for someone — a girl, no doubt, judging by the eager way his glance turned to the door every time it opened.

'Good evening,' Richard said.

Joe nodded. 'Rotten weather,' he rejoined.

'I suppose so.' Richard sipped. 'Will Matt be coming in?'

Joe took care in his reply. 'I think Matt's over at t'church.'

'Rehearsing again?'

'It's an important production. First time in years this play's been done by the kind of folks who used to do it – village folks, countrymen.'

'I won't intrude, then. I thought of having a talk with him, but I won't ... Tell him goodbye, will you?'

'Goodbye?'

'I'm leaving.'

Joe could only feel that it was all to the good if he did. Dolly was a changed girl since this man appeared on the horizon. Joe had nothing against him – he seemed decent enough, pleasant to talk to and all that. But it was interesting to recall that his mother had dropped the topic earlier this evening the minute Richard's name was mentioned. There'd been a coolness about her manner.

As if he could read Joe's mind, Richard said: 'I spoke to your mother this morning.'

'Oh?'

'She made me feel ... Well, I've decided it will be better if I clear out.'

Joe couldn't prevent the question. 'Does Dolly know?'

'I'll get a word with her later.'

But that proved more difficult than he thought. Dolly had work to do, and Amos made sure she did it. Only when half an hour had gone by did he get a chance to catch her eye.

'I'm here on purpose to speak to you, Dolly. You might make some effort.'

'Richard, we can't talk in t'bar. I've work to do.'

'Where, then?'

'What do we need to say to each other? It's all been said.'

'Not by any means. And once I've had it out with Matt –'

'Richard, please! Please don't drag Matt into this!'

Her voice had carried through the general chatter of the pub. Amos approached. 'Owt wrong?' he asked.

'No, everything's quite all right, Mr Brearley.'

'I thought I heard you –'

'Look here, Mr Brearley,' said Richard, 'would it put you out a lot if I had a word in private with Dolly?'

Amos was shocked. 'In working hours?'

'Surely she's entitled to some sort of break? It's after nine. She's been here since ... when? ... five?'

'Miss Acaster knows her conditions of employment, thank you, Mr Roper.'

'We only want a few minutes.'

Amos was about to say an emphatic no, but something about the strain in Miss Acaster's face made him change his mind. 'All right, then,' he said. 'But don't forget we get a bit of a rush about nine-thirty, usually.'

Dolly was far from feeling grateful. The last thing she wanted was a tête-à-tête with Richard. But there was nothing for it. She fetched her coat and slipped out.

He opened the door of the Citröen for her, closed it after her, then himself got in in the driver's seat.

Neither of them spoke at first. Then Richard said, 'I feel I have to speak to Matt. I'm going away for Christmas – up to Scotland, to relations. I don't want him to think I'm clearing out and leaving him a clear field.'

'Oh, Richard!'

'He's over at the church, I hear.'

'Please don't. Don't involve him. He doesn't even know ... He didn't know you existed. He ... there was no reason to tell him.'

'Are you saying there's nothing between you?'

She couldn't say that. She was silent.

'Don't you think we owe it to him to set him straight?'

'You know it's nothing like that on your part. You just want to hurt him. Richard – please – if I promise –'

'What?'

'To see you when you come back from Scotland? If I agree to let you have your say to the full ...'

'There's no chance here.'

'I'll come and meet you.'

'Where?'

'At Brassington, where you've been staying. The Red Lion.'

86

She saw his hands on the wheel relax, and she knew he felt he had won a great point. She was furious with herself — but what else could she do? At all costs she must keep Matt out of this.

'All right,' he said. 'I have to be at a wedding in Perth on January 3rd. Next day? At the Red Lion?'

'At the Red Lion. Now I must get back, Richard.'

'Oh, come on —'

Before he could stop her she had opened the door and scrambled out. She hurried to the back door of the inn. He strode after her. As she reached the entrance he caught her sleeve. 'You promise?'

'I promise.'

'The Red Lion Brassington, on the 4th January?'

'I'll be there.'

He would have said more, but her employer was already at the door in search of her. 'Miss Acaster, if you wouldn't mind?' he said. 'I am paying you, if you recall.'

'I'm coming.'

Amos was about to follow her in when Richard called him back. 'Mr Brearley.'

'Yes? I'm rather busy, Mr Roper.'

'I just wanted to give you this.'

'Eh?' Amos found he was accepting a currency note. 'What's this for?'

'For Miss Acaster's time.'

'Mr Roper!'

'Well, say it's for the staff Christmas box, then,' Richard flung over his shoulder as he walked away.

Amos didn't know whether to be offended or pleased. It was a pound note. But then ... Staff Christmas box! He was the staff, he and Miss Acaster and Mr Wilks. He and Mr Wilks were joint owners, above such things as tips. And as to Miss Acaster ... Surely a gentleman wouldn't offer tips to his young lady?

Baffled, Amos went into the bar. After a moment's thought, he put the pound note in a net Christmas stocking hanging from the till, asking for aid to spastic children.

Dolly had hung up her coat and got straight to work. She

was serving a roistering group from a Young Farmer's Club. After a bit the urgency was over and Amos approached her. He was going to say something to her about the money, in case Mr Roper ever mentioned it to her.

But Dolly forestalled him. 'Mr Brearley, I wonder if you'd agree to let me have time off over Christmas?'

'You'll have the usual break periods –'

'No, I meant, could I have a few days? I ... er ... I'd like to go home to spend it with my mother. She needs me.'

'Indeed?'

'I think I told you – she's an asthma sufferer.'

'I believe you mentioned it, Miss Acaster.'

'If you've no objections, I'd like to spend Christmas with her.'

'Mm ...'

'It's a bit sudden. I'm sorry.'

Amos stroked his sideboards. 'Happen it isn't such a surprise.'

'What do'you mean?'

'Well, really, Miss Acaster, I've felt for some time that your mind hasn't been on your work. Ever since Mr Roper appeared, in fact.'

'I'm sorry.' She hesitated and began again, 'It's this way –'

'Don't tell me owt,' Amos said, holding up a hand. 'I don't want to know your affairs, Miss Acaster. My duties as a reporter give me a certain insight into folk's characters, and I must say for some day now you've simply not been with us.'

'I didn't mean to be –'

'To tell the truth, I'll be quite glad to have my premises in better hands over the festive season. Don't concern yourself about leaving me in the lurch. A man with my experience of innkeeping is never at a loss.'

'It's just that I feel I've got to get away!'

'Oh, quite. Never mind other folk's arrangements! But that's the way the world is these days. Nobody can be relied on any more. But I won't worry you with my opinion. I can see the matter's all settled, really. My permission's just a formality.'

'I can go, then?'

'For how long?'

'I thought ... A week, happen?'

'From when?'

'From Christmas Eve?'

Amos did some calculations. That didn't bring her up to the date of the appointment with Mr Roper at the Red Lion. It meant she'd be back on the 31st, New Year's eve, looking white and scared, and worrying her way through until four days later. He was on the point of saying, generously, 'Take two weeks.' But then he thought about the usual pressure of work over New Year, and how the dusting would be neglected, and no one to make good coffee, and he held his tongue.

'Very well,' he said. Then, rather to his own surprise, he added: 'It's to be hoped the break will do you good.'

The unexpected kindness – or the relaxation in his disapproval – was so unexpected that Dolly's eyes filled with tears. She gave him a strange, helpless smile.

To his amazement, Amos felt quite upset.

In the church, the rehearsal was breaking up. Mr Hinton was looking pleased. 'It's coming along, coming along.'

'But where to?' asked Matt. 'I can hear that we're saying words, but are we making ourselves understood?'

'You'd be surprised, Mr Skilbeck. Those words, medieval though they are, are so like present-day Yorkshire dialect that they came over very well if they're said simply.'

'Aye,' said Matt without conviction. His fair short hair was covered in a headdress made of white cotton held in place with a twisted cord of brown and red. He didn't look the least bit Eastern, but he was doing his best. Mr Hinton had insisted the 'shepherds' wear their headdresses this evening because they had to pass under an arch at the side of the chancel, intended to be the entrance to the stable, and he was afraid they'd catch on the 'ivy' dangling down from it.

'That's a danger, is that,' Annie said to him, rising from her place among the pews. 'I think we'd be better without it.'

'But Mrs Mallsley has taken such pains to tack that ivy on the arch!'

'I meant, we'd be better without the arch altogether, Mr Hinton.'

'But it's the entrance to the stable.'

'But we know the manger is in a stable, Mr Hinton. We don't have to come "in" and "out" – we can take all that for granted.'

'You know, I believe you're right!' The vicar beamed at her. '"Simplify, simplify", as Henry Thoreau said. We'll leave the arch out of the production.' He clapped his hands for attention. 'Well, thank you, everyone. It went well. Same time tomorrow evening?'

'Yes, vicar.'

'All right, but I'll be a bit late.'

'I'll have to get a lift.' The usual last minute arrangements were going ahead. The vicar said to Annie, 'Is Mr Pearson nearly ready with the lamb?'

'I think he's just putting the finishing touches to it now. If I remember rightly, he glued on the fleece early this morning and was waiting for it to dry.'

'You're all so helpful ...'

When Matt had got rid of his Arabian gear and found his coat, he joined Annie. He had the Land-Rover in the lane outside the churchyard. When they were on the way to Emmerdale he said, 'I thought Dolly would have dropped in this evening.'

'Probably couldn't get away.'

'I'll come back and fetch her home later on.'

'Matt ...'

'Aye?'

'You think a lot of Dolly, don't you?'

'Of course I do.' He thought about what she had told him of her past, and added inwardly, 'No matter what ...'

'I think she needs to know that, just at the moment, lad.'

'You mean, because of this Roper?'

'He's dangerous. He doesn't understand that other people have feelings.'

Matt glanced at her. It was rare for his mother-in-law to express criticism of another human being. The mere fact that she did so filled him with anxiety. He knew Roper was dangerous – he felt outclassed, outdistanced by him. If Annie was warning him to keep his defences up against him, it meant Richard had given her reason to be afraid.

'Has he been bothering you?' he said, in a hardening tone.

'We had a talk. I tried to tell him ... But he's not the sort to listen, Matt.'

'If only Dolly would say she'd like to have him thrown out –'

'She can't do that, Matt. She's afraid of driving him to do summat silly.'

Indoors, Sam was putting the final touches to the lamb. It was a strictly symbolic lamb, rather flat and rectangular, but the fleece was white and fluffy.

'Hey-up,' said Matt, 'if any of the ewes gave birth to owt like that, I'd call t'vet!'

Sam was offended. 'It's so you can carry it easy. Go on, pick it up. You'll see. It just fits into the crook of your arm snug as ploughshare in furrow.'

For a space they admired the lamb and talked about the rehearsal. Then Matt, who had only unbuttoned his jacket, got up. 'I'll fetch Dolly.'

'She's got the scooter –'

'I'll sling it in the back of Land-Rover. Rotten weather for riding a scooter, Grandad.'

'Aye, right enough,' Sam agreed, having realised that in any case he ought not to put forward commonsense when a man was trying to get a moment alone with a girl.

When Dolly came out of the Woolpack, Matt tooted to let her know he'd put her scooter on the vehicle. He opened the door to let her climb in. There was a little film of moisture over her coat and her soft, bouncy hair. Behind her was the sound of Amos locking up the Woolpack for the night.

'You didn't come to the rehearsal,' he said as he pulled away.

'No. We got busy.'

'Mr Hinton's decided to do away with the arch and the ivy.'

'Oh. Happen that's best.'

'Dolly –'

'I'm going away, Matt.'

'What?'

'Going away. For Christmas. I won't be here to see the play.'

'But ... but ... you've put so much into it ... the costumes ...'

'It doesn't matter.'

There was a long hesitation, then he said, 'Your friend Richard Roper?'

'He'll be gone too,' she replied.

'I see.' So that was it. Richard had won. He was taking Dolly away over Christmas.

There seemed nothing more to be said.

CHAPTER SEVEN

Joe had had a tiff with Lesley Gibson. It was all about who should go where at Christmas. Lesley was with her grandparents, who had bought Hawthorn Cottage. 'Naturally, they'll expect me to be there on Christmas Day for dinner – what time will you be there?'

'I shan't be there,' Joe said in surprise. 'I'll be at Emmerdale.'

'But I've told Granny and Grandad you'll be dining with us.'

'Nay, Lesley, Ma expects me to have Christmas dinner at Emmerdale. She's got goose and all the trimmings. It'd be far better if you came to us – Ma's catering for me and Grandad and Matt and Henry and Amos –'

'Well, that means she's got far too much to do –'

'Not a bit. One more would hardly be noticed. We'll expect you about two o'clock.'

'Two o'clock?' she said in astonishment.

'In the afternoon. Takes a while to roast a goose.'

'Oh, I see. Oh well, look – if you have to be at midday dinner with your mother, that's okay. You can come to us for dinner at eight.'

'But Lesley, we generally have a bit of a sing-song –'

'Well, so do Granny and Grandad. Carols round the piano.'

'Look, why can't we do it t'other way round? You come to two o'clock dinner with us, then I'll run you home for the evening meal with your grandparents.'

'Don't be absurd, Joe. I couldn't eat two Christmas dinners!'

'Well, what makes you think I could?'

'But you're a man.'

That hardly seemed to make sense. They couldn't come to any agreement so they parted with some coolness. Joe went home to sound out his mother about Christmas; if, by any chance, she seemed likely to take it in her stride that he wanted to be elsewhere, he might go to Hawthorn.

'What're we doing on Christmas Day?' he inquired that evening, dropping in on her before heading for bed at Demdyke.

'Oh, just the usual.' She laid aside her mending. 'Joe, it's going to be a bit touchy, this Christmas. I'd been counting on Dolly being here, but she's decided to go home to her mother.'

'Oh.'

'Matt's right down about it.'

'Yeah.' Well, that seemed to put paid to any idea of pulling out.

Dolly moved about between Emmerdale and the Woolpack like someone in a dream. Annie spoke gently to her at all times. The slightest roughness might have done away with that fragile composure, which Dolly valued so dearly. Matt seldom spoke these days. Joe, who had had hard times himself, knew he was suffering but was powerless to help.

'Happen things'll be better when she comes back,' he remarked.

Matt shrugged.

'It's not for long, after all, Matt. Just a week or so. And

she's not fond enough of her mother to want to stay on longer, from all I hear.'

Matt whirled, dropping the hay fork. 'She's going to her mother's?'

'Well ... aye, that's what Amos says.'

'I didn't know that.'

'Where d'you think she was going, then?'

'I ... I dunno. I just thought ...'

'Amos says her mother's had an asthmatic attack.'

But the flush of hope was dying in Matt's face. 'Aye,' he said. 'It makes a good reason to go.'

'Are you saying you think there's some other reason?' Joe persisted. 'I mean, Dolly's a straight lass. Why would she say it's her ma, if it isn't?'

Matt sighed and shook his head. Joe gave up.

He was worried about his brother-in-law. It was so unusual to see Matt other than equable and good-tempered that the crease of anxiety between his brows these days seemed like a bruise, a wound. 'Now Richard Roper's gone,' he said to his mother, 'you'd think Matt would be happier.'

'I don't think Matt can ever be happy if Dolly's not around,' Annie replied.

'It's as serious as that?'

She made no reply. 'The trouble is,' she murmured, 'to be sure if that's how Dolly feels.'

'Oh, she's right fond of him. Anyone can see that!'

'Anyone but Matt,' Annie sighed. 'He's too lacking in conceit to take it for granted she cares about him.'

'Hang it, why don't we just gang up on him and tell him?'

'What good would that do?' she demanded. 'While Dolly's still got to solve the problem of Richard Roper.'

'Ma ... is he a real problem? I mean, more than just a persistent old flame?'

'He's a problem, Joe. But he's Dolly's problem.'

Joe could only accept her judgement.

Joe's grandfather had his troubles too, but they were well known to the entire family. The day was approaching when the Butterworth Ball would have to be produced and handed over to Fred Teaker for temporary removal to the Miller's Arms. Fred Teaker had been to corner Sam at a committee meeting of the cricket group in the pavilion.

'I'll tell you summat, Sam Pearson,' he announced, 'I've had a look at that mucky ball in the Woolpack, and I know what you're up to! If you don't hand over the genuine Butterworth Ball to me for the 21st, it'll mean real trouble!'

For once in his life, Sam could think of nothing to say. He hastened to the Woolpack to report to Amos. Amos could only think of one thing to say: 'Oh, heck!'

'Look, why don't you make a clean breast of it?' suggested Henry. 'Tell 'em what actually happened. Somebody stole the Butterworth Ball, we were all in a tizzy, we put up another one as a temporary fill-in till we got the real one back.'

'Henry!' cried Sam. 'Do you think they don't know all that? I bet you what you like Fred Teaker's got the Butterworth Ball in his back parlour right this very minute, waiting to produce it in triumph after he's beaten us to our knees.'

'Oh, come on, Sam –'

'Beaten us to our knees?' echoed Amos. He was picturing the indignity. 'We've got to do summat!' he exclaimed.

Sam went home to rack his brains. Amos supervised the opening of the Woolpack for midday drinking. Henry, seeing the sun at last winking through the clouds, stepped out for a moment to fill his lungs with cold air.

Walter surged in as the door opened. A few others filtered in. Dolly was busy for a minute and was taken by surprise when a voice she'd never heard before said: 'I'll have a gin and coke, please.'

Not only a strange voice, but a strange drink. No one had ever asked for that before. Dolly surveyed the newcomer. She was a pretty girl with the latest dark lipstick and matching nail varnish.

When she brought the gin and the bottle of coke, the girl was studying the ball in the niche above the bar. 'That the famous Butterworth Ball?' she asked.

'I don't know about famous,' Dolly said, unwilling to tell an outright lie.

95

'It's famous in Robblesfield. They talk about it a lot.'

'You from there?' Dolly asked.

'No . . . I got a boyfriend lives there.'

'Oh?'

Lily Kimber waited to see if the barmaid would ask who. She was waiting to produce the name of Little Teaker, and see what effect it would have. But the barmaid refused to be drawn, even though Lily lingered over buying a hot pie to go with her gin and coke.

At length, tired of playing footsie, Lily inquired, 'Who's the owner here?'

'There are two, actually. Mr Brearley and Mr Wilks.'

'Just tell 'em I'd like a word with 'em, will you?'

That certainly had an effect. 'What, both of them?' Dolly exclaimed.

'Or one, or the other – I don't mind. Just tell 'em.'

'Now?'

'Now's as good a time as any.'

Perplexed, and after a glance to ensure there was no likelihood of anyone wanting anything in the bar for a moment, Dolly went into the back room. Amos and Henry were having their midday meal – pork chops, brussels sprouts and potatoes. 'Excuse me, Mr Brearley . . .'

'This is our dinner break, Miss Acaster,' Amos interrupted, his mouth full of potato which, however, didn't prevent him from sounding magisterial.

'I think it's important. There's a young lady in the bar asking to have a word.'

'A word? With who?'

'You or Mr Wilks. Or both.'

Henry raised his eyebrows. 'One young lady?'

'Yes, Mr Wilks.'

'Who is she?'

'I don't know, Mr Brearley.'

'Did you ask the name?'

'I didn't think it would help. She's a stranger.'

'Shall I—?' said Henry, laying aside his fork.

'I'll go, Mr Wilks. If it's trouble, I have more experience.'

But out in the bar, Amos was greeted by a young lady who was indeed a stranger, yet who nevertheless greeted him with a friendly smile.

'Mr Wilks? Or Mr Brearley?'

'I'm Mr Brearley, the licencee. What can I do for you, Miss . . .?'

'Miss Kimber, Lily Kimber. Can I have a word with you in private?'

Amos drew back. It was always his instinct to stay away from private words with female persons. 'We're private enough here.'

'I don't think so.' She leaned towards him. 'It's about the Butterworth Ball.'

That had the desired effect. Amos leapt to the flap, lifted it, and ushered her at once past the counter into the parlour. Henry, caught with his mouth full of half-chewed pork, rose politely.

Amos performed introductions in a voice that didn't actually quake. 'Miss Kimber wishes to speak to us about . . . er . . . that important matter.'

'What important matter?' Henry said, swallowing the pork and looking puzzled.

'*You* know.'

Henry didn't, and was far from associating a pretty young girl with the finaglings of the Robblesfield Cricket Team. But nods and becks and raised eyebrows on Amos's part forced him to the conclusion that he ought to look knowing. 'I see,' he said.

'Take a chair, Miss Kimber?' Amos said, offering her Henry's. He himself sat down in the chair he'd left when Dolly called him. Henry, miffed, picked up the lager he'd poured himself to help down the over-grilled pork.

'Cheers,' he said to Lily. She raised her gin-and-coke to him.

'You said you wished to . . . er . . . expropriate concerning the item in question?' Amos said.

'Eh?' said Lily.

'I think you mean expatiate, Amos,' Henry put in. 'You

97

want to clear something up, Miss Kimber?'

'Nowt o't'sort,' she returned promptly. 'I want to make some money.'

'Really?' Henry had always been one to catch on quick. 'You've something to sell?'

'Information.'

'Ah.' Henry set down his glass. 'About what?'

'T'Butterworth Ball.'

'You know where t'Ball is?' That was a surprise. She didn't look the type who'd do a good job on a burglary, and anybody who'd drink a mish-mash like gin-and-coke wasn't likely to make away with two-thirds of a bottle of whisky – straight whisky, from the bottle.

'I think I do. At least, I know where he said he put it.'

'Who?'

'Little Teaker.'

'Ah,' said Henry again. 'You're a friend of his?'

She shook her glass so that the coke made little brown bubbles rise to a fine froth at the top. 'You could say so,' she replied.

'Come on then,' Amos interrupted, almost beside himself with urgency. 'Tell us where it is.'

'Oh, well ... As I said ... nothing's for nothing in this world. I had to come here from Hotten on the bus.' She held up her glass. 'And I've had other expenses.'

'How much?' Henry asked.

Amos leapt up. 'Mr Wilks! She's trying blackmail!'

'I think you're right, Amos.'

'Does she really think we'll pay money to know the where-abouts of something that's rightly ours?'

'I think she does.'

'I'm not paying one penny, Mr Wilks!'

Lily smiled and got up. 'Well, if you won't, Mr Teaker will.'

'Fred Teaker?'

'That's right.'

'If his brother has it, how comes Fred doesn't know where it is?'

''Cos Little won't tell him. Little can't stand him. He was

going to, mind you, if the price was right. He told Fred he'd taken t'Ball, and dangled the idea in front of him of having it in t'place of honour for his daft centenary display, but Fred wouldn't come up wi' the cash. Then he started to get stroppy – Fred, I mean – trying to put the strong arm on Little. So Little's scarpered to London until after Christmas. And I'm the only one as knows where t'Ball is.'

'I'm not paying one penny,' Amos said. 'Blackmail's against t'law.'

'I can't see any law being broke,' Lily murmured. 'Can you, Mr Wilks?'

'She's right, Amos – she's not blackmailing us, she's offering to sell us a service –'

'Mr Wilks, I am not one as buys anything from young women –'

'But this is a special case –'

'I have my principles, Mr Wilks.'

Lily drank off the remains of the goo in her glass. She set it down with a slight bang. 'Suit yourself,' she said. 'I'm off to see Fred. But I don't like him, so I gave you first offer.'

'Now hang on,' pleaded Henry.

'Don't try to detain her,' Amos said, with fierce dignity. 'I don't want her sort under my roof –'

'But at least let's talk about it –'

'No amount of talk is going to make any difference. You can call it offering a service or payment for casual help, but I know what it really is and my conscience would never let me rest.'

'Amos!' Henry implored. He had gone past the immediate scene and was picturing Lily giving the information to Fred Teaker. If that happened, their goose was cooked. The Butterworth Ball would go on display at the Miller's Arms, the whole world would know that in the first place the Woolpack hadn't taken enough care of it, that they'd been outwitted by the men of Robblesfield, and that if Beckindale ever won the Ball again, it would be better safeguarded at the Malt Shovel. Henry and Amos would have to stand for unending jokes about it. The fact that it was a cricket ball which had figured in the episode lent itself to terrible puns which Henry would rather not even imagine.

He pulled himself together. The first priority was to deal with Amos's scruples. 'Listen, Amos, I understand how you feel. But if we just let Miss Kimber go, we've lost the chance to make her see the error of her ways.'

'Here!' Lily said, much affronted.

Henry, standing behind Amos, gave her a huge wink.

'Well,' Amos said, 'there is that.'

'You can talk to the lass, Amos. Make her see it's her duty to do the right thing.'

Lily looked as if she was about to give her opinion of that but paused on receiving another wink from Henry. Amos was looking at her, less unfriendly. She said: 'Well, you know ... I've always respected older men.'

'Sit down and have another drink, my dear. You'd like that, wouldn't you?'

'I ... er ... Well, why not?' She held out the glass. 'Gin and coke.'

Henry took care not to be near enough to take the glass. Amos accepted it, not exactly unwillingly. 'I'll tell Dolly,' he said, moving towards the door.

But Dolly was at the far end of the bar, and he had to go out. Henry whipped out his notecase. 'How much?' he demanded.

'Ten pounds,' said Lily.

'Five.'

'Nay,' said Lily. 'It's worth ten.'

'Oh, look here –'

'He'll be back in a minute.'

Defeated, Henry took out two fives. In a flash the notes had disappeared down the front neckline of Lily's clingy dress.

'Let him persuade you,' Henry said. 'You do it out of a change of heart, see? No money changes hands.'

'Piece of cake,' said Lily. 'My good instincts'll get the better of me.'

Amos reappeared as she was speaking. 'Good instincts,' he echoed, 'that's what I mean. We shouldn't trample them down.

It's a matter of principle, you see. T'Butterworth Ball belongs here. It was stolen. And honest folk always return stolen property. That's the law.'

'If it was stolen, I wonder you didn't bring in the law,' Lily said, unable to resist a little mischief. 'The police, I mean.'

Henry sent her a glance of desperation.

'We ... er ... felt that if we gave the thief time, his ... er ... conscience would make him return it,' Amos said.

'And meanwhile you put up a replica instead. I wonder your principles allowed you to do it.'

Amos was flummoxed. Henry said, 'That was to allow the thief time to *play his part*, Miss Kimber.'

'Oh aye. Well, you were very generous about it. You could have put Little in a lot o'trouble. Happen I owe you summat for that – being kind to Little.'

'Yes, you do!' Amos cried. 'We saved your boyfriend from prison, very likely!'

Lily smothered a grin. 'How could I have been so wicked as to come making things worse for you?' she said. 'I'll tell you where the Ball is. Little said he chucked it in t'vicarage garden.'

Amos was aghast. 'You mean ... a valuable relic like that ... he just threw it?'

'That's what he told me. Running past, he was, late at night. Suddenly it seemed daft to be carrying the thing. Heavy, is it, a cricket ball? Any road, he threw it over some laurel bushes.'

Dolly came in with a tray of drinks. Amazingly enough, Amos had ordered gin-and-coke for Lily, a half-pint for himself, and a scotch for Henry. It showed his state of mind that he didn't ask Henry for the price of the scotch there and then.

'Ta love,' Lily said, taking hers. 'Little said, he told Fred what he'd been up to but when Fred said "Give us t'ball, then", Little asked how much it was worth. One thing led to another, and Little got stubborn. So now he's pushed off to London to be out of the way.'

She took a deep swallow of her drink. Amos nodded at her in approval. When she set down the empty glass, he said, 'Wait a minute.'

'What for?'

He felt in his pocket. 'Just to show you that honesty really is t'best policy, here's a reward.' He produced a one pound note and handed it to her.

Lily took it, her eyes shining with delight. 'Oh, i'n't he nice?' she said to Henry. 'I never expected anything like this.'

'I know you didn't. I just wanted to show you it doesn't pay to be out for money all the time.'

Lily put the pound where the two fivers had gone. 'Well, then,' she said wistfully, 'happen I ought to be straight with you about the whole thing. Little told Fred where he threw the ball.'

'What?' shouted Amos and Henry in unison.

'That's why Little's gone to London. Fred sent him off so he wouldn't blab about it to anyone else.'

'Fred Teaker knows the ball's in the vicar's garden?'

'Aye. He's been here the last couple o'nights, looking for it.' She made for the door. 'Tara,' she said with a nonchalant wave of the hand.

Henry sat down in a heap. 'The scheming little minx!'

'Never mind that!' Amos cried, dismissing Miss Kimber's character as suddenly unimportant. 'Fred Teaker knows where the ball is! Happen he's found it already!'

With one accord, leaving their drinks untouched, they grabbed their coats and ran.

Luckily the rain had stopped and though the garden was sodden, it was possible to stoop over the plants without getting a deluge down your neck. But every twig, every bush, sent splashes over them. Before long trousers were soaked through, and soon after that, jackets too. The air was cold and raw. Wrists began to be red and roughened, fingers blackened by mud. Feet became heavier to move as mud caked their shoes.

They looked in the flower bed, they walked bent two-double over the lawn, prodding like starlings looking for worms. They plunged in among the half-shorn weeds, getting prickled by stinging nettles and caught by brambles.

'You go outside and be Little Teaker throwing the ball in,' Henry said at length. 'You run down the lane, you suddenly decide to get rid of the ball, and you chuck it into the garden.'

'Me?'

'Yes.'

'Play the part of a criminal?'

'Well, I'll do it, then. You stand here and check where the ball would have fallen.'

Henry went out and trotted down the lane. After about ten steps he tossed an imaginary ball into the air, caught it, then threw it. He trotted on, then turned and ran back, going in at the lane gate of the garden.

'Well?' he said.

'Well what?'

'Where do you think the ball landed?'

'How do I know?'

'But didn't you watch to see where it might have fallen?'

'You can only catch glimpses through the bushes. You should have called out when you were going to throw it and then I'd have watched.'

'Oh, Amos,' groaned Henry. 'I'll go and do it again. This time I'll call out.'

'Very well, Mr Wilks.' Amos stood like a sentinel waiting. When he heard Henry call Now!' he looked up. He saw nothing.

Henry appeared. 'Well?'

'I didn't see anything land.'

'Amos, I didn't throw anything! But judging by where I was when I called out, where do you think it might have gone?'

Amos said a surprising thing. 'Depends on the trajectory,' he said.

'Eh?'

'How much force – what angle.' Amos mused. 'I'm ex-Artillery, you know.'

'Bye, Amos, you're right! I'll find a pebble in the lane and

I'll throw that. That'll give us some idea of the trajectory.'

Once more Henry trotted down the lane, called 'Now!' and threw the pebble with a fairly casual movement. He came back into the garden.

'Among the weeds,' Amos said. 'But, sitha, that were only a small pebble. About half t'size of a cricket ball, if that.'

'Well, it was the first one I saw.'

'You should have looked for something about the right size.'

'Amos, there aren't many pebbles the size of a cricket ball – even in a country lane.'

'I'll go,' Amos said. 'I'll find something more like it.'

Off he went. A very long delay followed. Then his voice: 'This'll have to do. I'm going to throw it in a minute.'

Footsteps. The call of 'Now!' Nothing happened. Henry called 'Did you throw it?'

'Nay, Mr Wilks. I suddenly thought ... Overarm or under-arm?'

'*What?*'

'Well, it is supposed to be a cricket ball.'

'Eeh, lad, we're wasting time. It's getting dark. Come back in here and have a shufti, Amos.'

His partner reappeared and they resumed their search. At length Henry straightened, his hand in the small of his back. 'Oh, my lumbago!'

'I'm not too well myself, Mr Wilks.'

'Look here, let's use our heads. What did that lass say? He tossed it into the garden when he got fed up carrying it.'

'Aye.'

' "He ... threw it in ... over some laurel bushes," ' Henry quoted, dragging the words up out of his memory.

'That's it! That's it, Mr Wilks,' Amos agreed in excitement. 'It'll be the far side of the laurel bushes from the road.'

They glanced about in wild expectation.

There were no laurel bushes in the vicarage garden.

CHAPTER EIGHT

Sam shook his head at Henry and Amos. 'I could have told you there were no laurel bushes in that garden,' he said.

'That's all very well to say,' Henry mourned, 'but we took it for granted she was telling us the truth.'

'And I paid her a pound for it,' sighed Amos.

'Well, you wasted your money.'

'Nay. It can't be true. I mean, why should she come here with a pack of lies?'

'Put up to it by them Robblesfield lot.'

'No, Sam, I think she's quite the opposite – a bit fed up with them. Little Teaker's gone swanning off to London, and I think has left her a bit in the lurch. So came to us with her information. And I feel sure it's true Fred Teaker hasn't found the ball otherwise he'd be crowing over us.'

'That's right enough,' Sam agreed. 'They'd do anything, them lot.'

They were in the Emmerdale kitchen. You might say it was a council of war, except that they were sitting round the kitchen table eating ginger snaps and drinking hot tea.

Amos and Henry looked decidedly the worse for wear. They'd changed out of their wet clothes, but they had sundry scratches on cheeks and noses, raw-red wrists, and a weary air. Annie was comforting them in the only way she knew how, by tending the inner man.

'Little comes out of t'Woolpack,' Henry said. 'Runs down vicarage lane –'

'Staggers, more like,' put in Sam.

'Aye – staggers. Here, that's it. Why on earth did he go up vicarage lane anyhow? It's a dead end.'

'Mistook his way.'

'That's right! So he turns and comes back. Happen he threw the ball when he was coming *back*!'

'In which case,' Amos said, 'trajectory would have been quite different.'

'He comes back down the lane,' Henry said. 'It's a dark night ... I recall it were dark when we looked out.'

'Starlight,' Sam said. 'Bright stars. Frosty. My brussels got the benefit.'

'Starlight. He sees some bushes –'

'Not laurel bushes.'

'No.'

'Hey,' said Sam. 'What looks like laurel bushes in the dark?'

'What?'

'Rhododendrons!' said Annie. 'The vicarage garden has a whole row of them on the north side.'

'By heaven, that's where it is,' cried Henry, jumping up with renewed energy. 'We never thought to look that far in! But he threw it hard, that's it! Like you said, Amos – overarm! It was a cricket ball, after all.'

They made for the door. Sam got up and followed.

'Dad, you're not to go –'

'I'm going,' Sam said in a voice that brooked no opposition.

'But it's dark –'

'Give us a torch, then, Annie! Look sharp.'

And when she made no move, but seemed as if she'd detain him by catching at his jacket, he pushed past her, found a torch on the kitchen dresser, and almost ran out to scramble into Henry's car.

Annie went to the door. 'Don't stop there longer than ten minutes!' she called. 'You'll bring on your sciatica!'

But the car was already moving off and her voice was drowned in the sound.

Joe and Matt came in from the evening milking. They washed, before the evening meal. The meal was ready, but still Sam didn't come.

'They must be combing every inch of the garden,' Joe said, trying not to laugh. 'I wonder what the vicar thinks of it all?'

'He's at the church taking the choir through the carols for

the play,' Annie said. 'But any road, he's used to having folks ...'

'What?'

'Joe, go down to the vicarage and tell your grandfather to come home at once for his tea.'

'Ma, you know it's no use me going. He'll pay no heed.'

'You go. Tell him I know where Butterworth Ball has gone.'

'You what?' Joe said.

Even Matt, who seemed abstracted these days, looked round at her. 'You know?'

'I think I do. And by the time Grandad's home, I'll have it sorted out.'

Joe said: 'You'd better be right. He'll skin us all alive if you drag him away on a pretext.'

Joe drove down to the village in his own car. Henry's car was already parked in the vicarage lane. The headlights were on, to aid the search. Joe looked at the scene with some amusement. Henry, Amos and his grandfather were poking about among the rhododendrons, getting soaked by the showers of moisture coming down from the shaggy branches.

'Grandad, Ma says you're to come home. She says she knows where the Butterworth Ball really is.'

All three men straightened and turned as one. In the mottled light cast by the car headlights shining through the twigs and plants, the scene looked unreal. 'Talk about the Three Wise Men,' murmured Joe. 'Come on, Grandad.'

'Annie knows?'

'So she says. So come on.'

'We're coming too!' Amos exclaimed. 'I mean ... that is ... if your ma won't mind.'

'It's like at the end of a detective story,' Joe said, ushering them ahead of him. 'Everybody collects in the library to hear whodunit.'

'We know whodunit,' Henry muttered. 'What we want to know is, where-hid-it.'

Annie was adamant that they all sit down to eat when they came in cold and wet. She made them shed their topcoats, take off sodden boots, and swallow several mouthfuls of hot

107

gammon and greens before she would say a word.

'Come on, Ma,' Matt urged. 'We'll all get indigestion from the anxiety!'

'The ball,' Annie said, 'was found by the Scout troop.'

'Eh?' yelled Sam, springing up.

'Sit down, Grandad! I rang Tippy Scrawbrook. His lads tidied up the vicarage garden the afternoon of the day Amos heard the intruder in t'Woolpack.'

'So Tippy Scawbrook's got the Butterworth Ball?' Henry said.

'No. Billy Luttercombe has it.'

'Who the devil – pardon me – who's Billy Luttercombe?'

'One of the scouts. Lives out by Kennet Sleeve, where the waterfall is. His father works for that Ministry of Defence thing.'

'Billy Luttercombe?' cried Sam. 'Thank the lord for that.'

'You're sure he has it?'

'Oh yes. Tippy said the boy showed the ball to him, said, "I've found it, sir, should I hand it in?" And Tippy said he could keep it since it was so old and bedraggled.'

'Bedraggled! The Butterworth Ball!' Sam was shocked.

'I'll drive up there and get it back –'

'Nobody,' said Annie, raising her hand, 'is going anywhere until this meal has been eaten and everybody has dry clothes on.'

'Er ... well ...' Henry hesitated. It was his nature to do things at once, but the gammon smelt so good, and there was treacle tart to follow. 'Happen you're right,' he agreed.

About an hour later, six-forty-five of a December evening, they set out for Kennet Sleeve. It was high on the moor, an isolated spot, the cottage renovated by the civil servant who could afford to bring electricity and mains water to it after it had been derelict for years. The waterfall which gave its name to the spot sparkled in the wan moonlight.

And the moonlight was the only light. There was no light in the cottage windows, and even the lantern swinging from a post at the gate and intended to light the traveller on his weary way, was out,

Henry and Sam clambered out of the car. Amos had felt it his duty to go back and supervise the care of the bar now that he knew for sure where the Butterworth Ball had come to rest.

In the silence the two men approached the cottage door. There was a bell push. Henry rang. Inside, chimes played 'Home Sweet Home'. But nobody came.

Henry rang again. 'Be it never so humble,' rang the chimes.

'Hi!' yelled Sam, and hammered on the door with his fist.

No answer.

'Mrs Luttercombe! You there? Anybody there?'

Utter silence. They heard the falling water of Kennet Sleeve only two hundred yards away.

'They're not in,' said Sam in disbelief.

'Well ... Christmas is coming on ... out shopping, happen.'

'Shops are shut now.'

'But if they've been to Leeds – they might still be on their way back. Or visiting friends, mebbe.'

'Aye. What shall us do?'

'Hang on a bit?' suggested Henry.

They hung on a bit, sitting in his car. If the heater was to be kept going, a window had to be left open a crack otherwise they might suffer from carbon monoxide poisoning. But Sam complained he was getting a stiff neck from the draught. By and by Sam said, 'Let's go and ask their neighbours when they're likely to be home.'

Their 'neighbours' were two miles down the road at Kennet Crossroad. 'The Luttercombes?' said Mrs Grant. 'They've gone away for Christmas.'

'Gone away?' moaned Henry and Sam.

'Back after New Year. He's a civil servant, tha knows. Gets a long holiday.'

'And Billy Luttercombe?'

'What about him?'

'Where's he?'

'Gone with them, of course.'

'Where? Where?'

'*I* dunno. South, somewhere, to visit their folks.'

Sam was minded to break in and search the cottage at Kennet Sleeve. Henry restrained him. 'There's been enough of that,' he sighed. ''Sides, we wouldn't know where to look. I mean, where does a thirteen year old boy keep an old cricket ball? In a drawer? Toy cupboard? Coal shed? Ma's broom cupboard?'

Fred Teaker had said he wanted the Butterworth Ball for the 21st December. 'That's day after tomorrow,' groaned Sam, clutching the back of his neck where the draught had made it stiff – or perhaps it was the tension of terror. 'We're sunk, Henry.'

Not quite. When they got back with the bad news, Sam's daughter once more rose to the occasion. 'All we have to do is ask Bessie Aspinall at High Corner.'

'Where does she come into it?' Henry inquired.

'Bessie is June Luttercombe's sister. If anybody knows where they've gone for Christmas, Bessie will.'

Sam took his daughter's hand in his. 'Eeh, Annie, Annie,' he said, 'you've a head on you!' He turned to go, but this time she forestalled him.

'Nay, now, Dad, it's past eight. You've been hopping about like a cricket on a hot hob . Sit thee down.'

'But I must –'

'No you must not. Bessie Aspinall doesn't need the both of you to speak to her.' She glanced at Henry. 'You won't mind going on your own, Henry?'

'Of course not.' To tell the truth, Henry preferred it. While he quite understood the urgency of the situation, he didn't see it in quite the same light as Sam. Henry had no intention of breaking and entering, or holding up anyone on the highway, to get back the Butterworth Ball. 'I'll just drop in on Amos –'

'Get straight off to High Corner,' Sam interrupted. 'I'll ring Amos.'

That showed how important it was. Sam would never use the phone if it could be avoided.

Joe was in the Woolpack with Lesley when the call came

through for Amos. He heard Amos say, 'Hello, Sam,' but then, contrary to his expectations, Amos's face fell. By the time the conversation was over, the cloud seemed to have lifted a little, but Amos Brearley could not be described as a picture of happiness.

'Summat wrong, Amos?'

'Your grandad says your ma's put them on the track again. The Luttercombes have gone away for Christmas but Annie's given them the name of a sister.'

'Bessie Aspinall – aye.'

'Henry's gone to get the address they've gone to.'

Joe wanted to know what good that would do. 'If Billy's left the ball indoors somewhere –'

'Somebody'll have a key. We can get in and take it back.'

'Suppose he's taken it away with him?'

'You don't think he has, do you?'

'Well, I dunno. It's a real old cricket ball, and if he's a keen cricket fan he might take it with him on holiday, have a few goes pretending he's Botham.'

'Oh, heck,' said Amos.

'Don't tease him,' Lesley murmured to Joe when Amos had moved off to serve someone else. 'He takes it all in deadly earnest.'

'He's not the only one. There'll be war if that ball doesn't turn up.'

'Hm,' said Lesley. 'Hosilities haven't exactly ceased about our Christmas arrangements.'

They hadn't quite quarrelled, but every time the topic was mentioned a chill fell on them. They had decided that the only thing to do was to separate for Christmas. Lesley would spend it with her grandparents at Hawthorn, Joe would be with his family at Emmerdale. It wasn't what either of them wanted, but there seemed no other way.

'Peace, goodwill to all men,' Joe said.

'Humph! When the angels announced that, the British Christmas hadn't been invented!'

If Joe was worrying about Christmas, Matt had other things on his mind. The performance of the Nativity Play was draw-

111

ing near and with it the day when Dolly would leave Beckindale for the holiday.

Annie watched with sympathy while Matt wrestled with the problem. She was powerless to help. While the fate of Dolly's child could be changed by some wild action of Richard Roper's, no one ought to interfere.

Meanwhile the lesser activities of the village continued. The children's Christmas party would take place on December 28th, which would allow plenty of time for the excitement of Christmas Day with all its presents to die down.

As always, to finance the party, various schemes had been afoot. There had been a coffee morning, a sale of work, and now there was to be a jumble. The committee organising the jumble sale was under the chairmanship of Mrs Downs, but somehow Annie seemed to be constantly in demand over details – would there be enough trestle tables, had Willie Ockroyd agreed to lend his van, was the nursery contributing seedling pot plants same as last year?

Annie was on the telephone when Henry reappeared at Emmerdale. It was late for a visit. He looked apologetic, tired, and helpless.

'Bessie Aspinall says her sister and family have gone to his parents outside Torquay.'

'Aye?'

'Annie, they're not on t'phone.'

Annie was thankful that her father, nigh dropping with fatigue, had gone to bed half an hour since. 'Oh, Henry!'

'Mrs Aspinall knows nothing about the cricket ball. Billy never mentioned it to her. She's no idea whether he still has it, or what.'

'What's to do now, then?'

'Amos will creep into a corner and die.'

'He'll take it to heart, that's certain.'

'It's all so daft, Annie! It's only an old cricket ball.'

'Aye, but you could say that about so many things. "It's only a plain gold ring" – but no woman would part with her wedding ring.'

'This is less to do with sentiment and more to do with

112

village rivalry, Annie.'

'Do you think I don't know that? And my father's not blameless. When it comes to Robblesfield, he has a blind spot. If he has to admit the Butterworth Ball has been lost, he'll die of shame.'

'I should have taken Amos seriously that night. I should have dashed out the door – I might have caught up with Little Teaker.'

She smiled. 'I can just see you tackling Little Teaker, you in your dressing-gown and he half seas over with whisky.'

'Aye ... well ...' Henry gave a rueful grin. 'There's only one thing for it. I'll have to go to Torquay and see the Luttercombes.'

'Henry! With Christmas coming on? Haven't you things of your own to do?'

He shrugged, and for a moment looked lonely. 'Not as much as you'd think, Annie. There's the Nativity Play, of course, but I'll be back in time for that, and somebody else can take over the lighting if I'm a bit late.'

'When will you go?'

'Now's as good a time as any. I can catch a train in an hour's time and be in London by three-thirty am. I dunno what the connections are like but I reckon there'll be a train to Torquay about seven. I ought to be there before midday. Once I know the news about the ball, I'll ring Amos – that should be some time tomorrow afternoon. I'll come straight back, should be in good time for the play on the following day.'

'You'll be exhausted.'

'All in a good cause.' He nodded at her and hurried out. She went after him to call a warning about driving with care, but he was gone.

She felt she ought to ring Amos to put him in the picture. The reaction was what she might have expected: dismay, consternation, and some resentment. 'You mean he's just gone off, like that? Leaving me to cope in t'bar?'

'You've got Dolly, Amos –'

'She might as well not be here, she's that quiet and listless.'

113

'Well, Henry plans to be back late tomorrow night or early next morning, I think.'

'And we're to wait until then –'

'He says he'll ring as soon as he has news.'

'He'd better, because day after tomorrow, Fred Teaker will be here demanding the ball.'

'I know, Amos. Henry's doing all he can.'

There was a sense of suspended animation over everything next day. Amos never strayed far from the telephone, and each time it rang he leapt to it as if it might jump out of the Woolpack if he didn't catch it at once. Midday opening came and went. Sam came in to have a half of cider. 'Any news?' he muttered as he paid for it. And Amos gloomily shook his head.

About four o'clock, when he had dozed off momentarily in a hard chair he had set by the phone, it rang. Amos leapt up.

'Amos? I've been trying to get through for half an hour!'

'I've been here, Mr Wilks! The phone never rang!'

'No, I mean, the lines have all been busy, I couldn't get a connection. Amos ... Billy Luttercombe says he was practising with the cricket ball in the playing fields behind the tennis court, and it went over into the allotments.'

'*What!*'

'He heard the tinkle of breaking glass. He thinks it went through somebody's cucumber frame. So he didn't go to look.'

'You mean ... He doesn't know where it went?'

'No idea.'

'Oh, heck!'

'I'm at Torquay Station now, Amos. There's a train in about half an hour. With luck I'll catch a connection in London that should get me to Leeds by two thirty in the morning.'

'Aye,' said Amos helplessly.

'Bye for now.'

'Mr Wilks!'

'What?'

'What are we going to *do*?'

114

'Pray, Amos. Pray.'

Amos wasn't one who knew much about prayer. He felt that was better left in the hands of Sam Pearson, who was a regular churchgoer. Sam took the news badly. 'We can try searching the allotments,' he said, 'but there's that many little shacks and bits of cold frames there, it would take a month.'

'We'll have to ask Fred Teaker to postpone his bi-centenary celebrations,' Amos suggested.

Sam only looked at him. Amos groaned. 'No, that wouldn't be any use,' he agreed.

Amos didn't sleep that night. But there were others in Beckindale who were awake through the night hours. Dolly Acaster was watching the moon move across the sky from her attic window. Below, in the bedroom he had shared with his dead wife Peggy, Matt Skilbeck slept and woke and slept and woke, haunted by dreams of the past and visions of the future. Annie was restless, thinking about the jumble sale which would take place in the afternoon at two, to be immediately followed by the Nativity Play's first performance at four. Henry was speeding towards Leeds in a rocking railway carriage, nodding off now and again but always jerking awake as his elbow slipped off the table.

He tumbled out at last at Leeds Central, feeling creased and unkempt and weary to the bone. His car was in a multi-storey car park. On his way there he stopped off at an all-night cafe for a very strong cup of sweet tea to nerve him for the drive home.

When he got to Beckindale he found that Amos, forgetting he was due in the wee small hours, had locked up. He was forced to hammer on the door. Amos appeared at length, grasping a poker and with his sparse hair on end.

'Oh, it's you, Mr Wilks!'

'Who did you think it was? The Queen of the Night?'

'Who?'

'Oh, never mind. Let's get locked up and off to bed. I'm absolutely dead.'

'Aye,' said Amos, trying to make up for his lack of sympathy hitherto, 'you look it.'

115

'Thank you, Amos, and goodnight!'

Surprisingly, Henry felt quite good the following day. He slept until ten, then rose determined not to be depressed. After all, the whole thing was a storm in a teacup. Just a daft village quarrel. He, Henry Wilks, retired businessman of Bradford, was not to be brought down to such a petty level.

By contrast, Amos had decided that the axe was about to fall. No French aristocrat getting ready for Madame Guillotine ever looked so ready for the end. 'He'll be here,' he said to Henry, 'probably by midday. I intend to appeal to his better nature.'

'You do that,' Henry said.

Dolly was giving the place a final clean so that it would last out over the Christmas period. The busy hum of the vacuum cleaner made a cheerful background to the conversation. 'What time's she going?' asked Henry.

'Dunno. Hasn't a word to say for herself these days, hardly.'

At opening time Amos unlocked the front door as if he expected Fred Teaker to storm in at once. But only Old Walter was there, as usual. The place was quiet. Sam came in about one.

'Any sign of him?'

'Not so far.'

'I couldn't eat my dinner! My stomach's in a knot.'

'This matter is taking its toll of all of us,' Amos said heavily.

'Come on, now, Sam,' Henry urged. 'It's not the end of the world.'

Sam looked at Amos, Amos looked at Sam. They both looked at Henry. He was quelled.

Time went by and still Fred Teaker didn't appear. 'He's hanging it out to get us right on edge,' Sam muttered. 'Just like them Robblesfield lot!'

'He's busy, happen,' Henry pointed out. 'He's a pub to run, just like us.'

Two o'clock came and went. Old Walter went home. The last few customers popped in. Closing time was near. There was some activity due to the jumble sale going on in the village

116

hall, but most of its customers were women and they, as a rule, were not habituees of the Woolpack.

At five and twenty past two, the door opened and Fred Teaker came in. With him was Constable Dewes, the patrolman for the district.

'Oh heck,' said Amos.

'That's a dirty trick,' Sam muttered.

Even Henry was taken aback. He hadn't expected legal proceedings.

'Now then,' said Constable Dewes, 'I'm making inquiries about the Butterworth Ball.'

Everybody glanced at the ball in the niche behind the bar.

'What inquiries?' Amos said in a trembling voice.

'I want to know what's been going on.'

'How d'you mean, going on?' Sam put in. 'What are you on about, Ted?'

The constable gave him a cool stare. 'You're in on it too, Sam. Nothing can happen to the Butterworth Ball except you'll be in on it.'

'What makes you think anything's happened to it?'

'Huh,' said Fred Teaker.

'From information received,' the constable began, 'I have reason to believe that there was a break-in on these premises and that the Butterworth Ball was stolen. Is that correct?'

'There was no break-in,' Henry said.

'Mr Wilks. I'd advise you to be careful what you say.'

'I'm being absolutely exact. There was no break-in.'

The constable half-turned towards Fred Teaker. Fred Teaker said: 'D'you deny that somebody got in here and took the Ball?'

'Some drunk slept it off in the gents,' Amos said. 'That's not a break-in. We didn't bother the police wi' it.'

'But the ball went missing?'

'Not exactly missing,' Sam said. 'This character threw it in the vicarage garden.'

The constable frowned. 'I ... er ... so you got it back?'

'Everything that could be expected was done to retrieve it.'

'Mr Wilks, is that the Butterworth Ball or isn't it?'

117

They all looked at the ball in the niche. No one dared speak. Then Sam drew a deep breath.

'Well, no, is isn't,' he admitted.

'Ah,' Fred Teaker said.

Constable Dewes surveyed them. 'You weren't going to tell me that, now were you?' he challenged. 'You were going to let on that that ball in the niche is the Butterworth Ball.'

'Nowt o't'sort!' Amos cried. 'That is only a temporary makeshift –'

'Temporary for how long?' Fred asked. .

'Until we can put the real one back.'

'And when will that be?'

Annie came in, the door being still unlocked although closing time was officially past. 'Is this what you're here about, Fred?' she asked in a cheerful tone, and held out her hand.

In it she was holding the Butterworth Ball.

After Fred Teaker had gone, baffled and chagrined and in some disgrace with Constable Dewes for wasting his time, she explained how she'd come by it. 'It was in a carton of jumble Willie Ockroyd collected on his van this morning. Last minute collection – and we don't know who the stuff came from. But somebody picked it up out of his cold frame and tossed it into the box of oddments for the sale.'

'Annie,' said Amos with fervent gratitude, 'I'll never forget this!'

She released her hand from his handshake. 'I must go,' she said. 'There's things to do still, and the Nativity Play begins soon.'

'I'll be over in a minute, Annie,' Henry promised. 'Tell t'vicar not to touch that big moveable lime – it'll topple.'

He beamed at her as she went out. She thought to herself, 'If only it was as easy as that to make everyone else happy.'

In the church, everything was a sort of orderly chaos. Frightened actors were in corners mouthing their lines to themselves. Mothers were tweaking angels' wings. The choir was in the vestry having a last run-through of the most difficult carol. Only Matt seemed perfectly calm.

It no longer mattered to him whether he knew the words

or not. He had learned them and could say them – and the embarrassment he had felt in the past at having to appear before the villagers of Beckindale was unimportant now. The play would begin, he would play his part. Stage-fright would be foolish. There were more important things in the world.

He had hoped against hope that Dolly would confide in him again. If she were going to meet Richard Roper for the holidays, that was of course her own affair – but he had somehow thought she might explain herself to him. Yet she was silent. She was avoiding him.

The congregation fell silent, the organ began its soft voluntary. Annie took her place at the back of the church. From this distance the 'stage' before the choir looked like a magic bower, bathed in soft light as the winter day faded, touched in colour, thanks to the work Dolly had done.

Dolly ... Annie got up and slipped out. She must bring Dolly to the church to see her handiwork.

Dolly was coming out of the Woolpack with the suitcase she'd brought from Emmerdale earlier. She intended to strap it on the scooter, but paused as Annie came up.

'Come and see the play, lass. It's just beginning.'

Dolly shook her head. 'I couldn't.'

'Come and take a look. Just listen to Matt say his first lines.'

'No.'

'Dolly – you are coming back?'

'I'm not sure.' She turned away her head. She didn't want Annie to see the tears that were welling up.

'But Matt expects you back, love.'

'Does he? I wonder if he does.'

'Haven't you and him discussed things?'

'Oh, discussed –!' Dolly threw out her hands. 'We don't find it easy to talk about some things. We're ... I don't know ... words don't come easy.'

Annie put a hand on her arm. 'You told him about the baby?'

'Yes.'

'About Richard wanting him?'

119

'No.'

There was a silence. 'Dolly ... suppose Matt's in love with you?'

Dolly turned tear-bright eyes upon her. 'What of it? What does that mean? I was in love with Richard once. I don't know if I put my faith in that any more.'

She pulled herself free of Annie's grasp, strapped the case on the carrier of the scooter, and sighed. 'You go back. Don't miss the play because of me.'

'My lass, I wish you'd come in with me.'

'No.'

Shaking her head, Annie turned to the church. She slipped in without disturbing anyone. Matt was centre stage, the loose robe somehow clothing him in austere majesty, the light from Henry's lime making the colours glow.

'"*Hayll, derlyng dere, full of Godhede!*
I pray thee be nere when that I have nede ..."'

The audience was rapt. Within the walls of the old church, an ancient magic was being recreated.

Yet in the distance Annie could hear the sound of Dolly's moped, carrying her away.

CHAPTER NINE

The Nativity Play had two performances, Saturday afternoon and Sunday afternoon. It seemed to hold Beckindale in its spell for those two days. The return to the ordinary world on Monday was painful, but Christmas was coming – Christmas was almost upon them.

The Reverend Donald Hinton seemed to raise his head and look around him. For two weeks at least, perhaps more, his entire mind had been taken up with the play – with setting it before the people of the village in all its majestic simplicity, in helping the participants to learn their lines, in trying to make clear to them and to himself what the speakers of five centuries ago had meant by those strange, powerful words.

Now it was done – triumphantly. Now he could say to himself, almost, 'Lord, lettest Thou Thy servant depart ...' Not quite! He still had work to do in his parish.

And he had an awful feeling he'd been neglecting it.

'Miss Acaster is comfortable and happy in her new lodgings, I hope?' he remarked to Joe Sugden, coming across him loading frozen food into the Landrover outside the village shop.

Joe paused, pushed a carton of frozen peas into a safer position in its surroundings, then turned to face the vicar. 'I think she's comfortable enough,' he said.

Mr Hinton gave a little frown. He was a very quiet, sensitive man, and he caught the nuance in what Joe said.

'Is something wrong?' he asked.

Joe pursed his lips. 'It's not for me to say. All I know is, Dolly's going through a very bad time.',

'Oh ... Nothing to do with the fact that I wanted her to leave the vicarage, I hope!'

'Nay, vicar, it's some personal thing.' Joe suddenly leaned towards him and spoke in a low, sad voice. 'She's going through a very bad time,' he said. 'I ... hate to see it. Because, you see, it makes Matt so miserable.'

'Perhaps ... I could have a word with her?' Hinton said, rather helplessly.

'She's gone, vicar.'

'Gone?'

'For the moment. Gone to stay with her mother, so far as we can gather.'

'You say that is if ... as if you think she's not really gone there.'

'I dunno. Was a time I'd have said you could rely on any word Dolly spoke.' Joe caught himself up. 'Of course she's gone to her ma. Natural, isn't it? For Christmas.'

'Oh, I see. She's coming back.'

Joe's dark eyes dwelt on the vicar's face. 'That's to be seen,' he said.

Hinton was appalled at himself. How could he have been so remiss? He had chased the poor girl out of his house because he preferred his own company, when it seemed she was having a personal crisis; and now, instead of turning to the priest for help, she had retreated who-knew-where without a friend to turn to.

He went into church — it was where he had been heading when he came across Joe loading his mother's Christmas supplies into the Landrover. But instead of setting about the practicalities of tidying up after the play. Hinton went to the altar and sank on his knees.

He could find no words to express his feelings, no prayer to send his plea upwards. But his whole being was saying: 'Forgive me, I let myself be led aside from my real work.'

Half an hour later he came out of the church and walked to the Woolpack. Amos was sweeping dust out of the front door.

'Good morning, Mr Brearley.'

'Morning, vicar.'

'Doing your own chores again, I see.'

'For t'time being.'

'Oh? Miss Acaster is coming back?'

Amos leaned on his broom. A momentary chill seized him. 'Any reason to think she won't?' he demanded.

'Not at all. I'm simply asking.'

'But I mean ... what made you ask? You haven't heard her say she was leaving the village for good?'

'I haven't had a moment's conversation with Miss Acaster for over two weeks,' Hinton said with shame.

'Oh.' Amos was a bit reassured. He began sweeping the motley little collection of cigarette ends, mint wrappings and crisp packets out into the street. Here the December breeze caught them and whirled them away.

Hinton said: 'Speaking as an environmentalist, I can't approve of that.'

'What?'

'Letting litter get blown about the village.'

122

'Eh?' Amos was affronted. 'It's traditional to sweep out the front every morning, vicar.'

'I'm sure it is.'

'I mean, the bits have got to go somewhere, haven't they?'

'Miss Acaster sweeps them all up into a dustpan and puts them in the bin,' Hinton said.

'Oh! Well, I were going to do that, o'course. But the wind took 'em off.'

'To be sure,' said Hinton. 'May I come in a moment?'

'Oh, please – this way.' Amos ushered him in. 'If it's to inquire about the piece I'm doing for the *Courier* about t'play, I can tell you I'm giving you a real write-up –'

'Thank you,' Hinton said. 'It wasn't that, but I do appreciate it. I came to say thank you to Mr Wilks for his help with the lighting. I hope to get round everyone before the duties of Christmas take up all my time and energy.'

'Oh, aye, of course, Mr Wilks played his part,' Amos said. 'But, vicar – I mean ... the story, and the way they put it over ... and the clothes ... and the sort of slow movements ... and ... and .. well ... I'd no idea.' Amos had been really overset by the play. He'd been treating the whole thing with some scorn until the moment he actually saw it. He wouldn't have known how to express it, but it had opened up a new world to him.

'You're very kind. The performance was a joint effort, of course. I do think that the actors surpassed themselves, though.'

Henry came downstairs. He'd been pottering about upstairs trying to think how to start his day. For the moment everything seemed to have gone flat, now that the play was over.

'Good morning, vicar,' he said with pleasure.

'Good morning, Henry. I've come to say a special thank you for all your work. Not least of which, I gather, was saving the entire village from a crisis on Saturday about some local trophy.'

'You've heard about that?' Henry said with a laugh yet with some alarm. He didn't want it noised abroad.

'Not in any detail,' said the vicar. 'But Mr Pearson men-

123

tioned to me yesterday after service that among those whom we ought to thank in our prayers for their services to our community was yourself. "Saved our bacon", I think was his phrase.'

'Oh, as to that,' Amos put in, 'I think credit where credit's due. Mrs Sugden was the one, really. I'll never forget what she did.'

Hinton smiled at them. It was cheering to find two people who were so pleased with life. After his long moment of intense self-doubt, they reassured him. But that brought him to the ulterior motive for his visit. 'Are you having anyone else in to do Miss Acaster's chores over the holiday?' he asked.

'Who could we get?' Henry said. 'We've been through all that, more than once. Lucky to get Dolly.'

Amos made a shrugging movement, not quite a negative. 'I've said my say on that point. I'm not totally against a female bar-person, but I'd hope we'd get better service than we've had from Miss Acaster this past two or three weeks.'

'I can't believe Miss Acaster has fallen short? While she was at the vicarage, she was a most industrious helper.'

'Oh, industrious all right. What I mean is, folks who come into an inn like a bit of a smile and a chat. But there, you can't expect a young woman to be able to carry out duties o'that kind the way a man of my years can do it.'

'You should come in here some evening when the darts club is meeting, vicar,' Henry said. 'Like a salon during the reign of the Sun King, it is – Voltaire and Rousseau left nowhere.'

'A good hostelry can make its way without foreign drinks,' Amos said loftily. 'I never feel any need to stock 'em.'

Mr Hinton felt guilty at joining in any teasing of Amos, but he couldn't help an inner smile at the idea of two of France's greatest philosophers dismissed as fancy foreign drinks.

'I very much want to thank Miss Acaster for her help with the costumes and scenery,' he said. 'When will she be back?'

There was a pause.

'If you want my opinion –'

'I'm sure the vicar's too busy to hear all that, Amos.'

'That's all very well, Mr Wilks, but it's very unsatisfactory not to know Miss Acaster's full intentions. If she's going to wed that young man, why don't she say so?'

'I think you've answered your own question. She isn't, so she doesn't.'

'Eh?'

'Miss Acaster's thinking of marriage?' inquired the vicar.

'Nay, not a bit –'

'Well, if she isn't, that Mr Roper is!' Amos interrupted. 'The way he goes on, it's signed, sealed and settled. And I must say Miss Acaster doesn't turn him away wi' quite the determination of a lass that intends to have nowt to do wi' him.'

Henry was silent.

'Are you saying that Miss Acaster may not come back at all?'

'Oh, she'll come back. There's stuff of hers here – and at Emmerdale, I've no doubt. But *my* opinion –' Amos cast a minatory glance at Henry –' is that she'll come back just to collect it and then she'll be off.'

'Oh dear. I'm sorry.'

After a few more moment's chat about the forthcoming festivities Mr Hinton withdrew. Henry came to the door with him and stepped out into the cold morning air.

'Don't attach too much importance to what Amos has been saying about Dolly, vicar. I'm by no means convinced she even likes this young Roper.'

'Really? But then why –'

'I don't understand it myself. I don't think anybody does, except happen Annie, and ... funnily enough, she seems powerless to help.'

'I've been very remiss,' Hinton said. 'I'd no idea there was a situation like this.'

'Don't blame yourself. Dolly is the kind to keep her troubles to herself. It's just that this lad Roper is quite the opposite – he's all open and honest, to listen to him. But there's a streak of something ... I dunno ...'

'He has talked of marriage? So that others took it up?'

'Oh aye. First thing he said, almost, was that she was his fiancée. Putting a claim on her, you might say.' Henry sighed. 'Not like Matt.'

'Yes,' said Mr Hinton. 'Matt . . .'

Matt Skilbeck wasn't a regular churchgoer in quite the same way as the Sugdens. Hinton felt he had unspoken doubts about religion – but then, what thinking man has not had doubts, Hinton said to himself. During the rehearsals of the play, the vicar had come to know and value Matt very highly. There was something strong, true and unchanging about Matt; he was like the land itself, calm and enduring.

Although he had recently been totally taken up with the production of the Nativity Play, the vicar had been in Beckindale long enough to get to know some of the basic relationships. One that had seemed to be going along very nicely was the friendship between Dolly Acaster and Matt Skilbeck.

During the rehearsals it had been pleasant to glance along the chancel and see them, two fair heads bent over the book, Matt's voice struggling with the words and Dolly's lighter, buoyant tones of encouragement.

To tell the truth, the vicar had taken it for granted . . . Well, now he found he was wrong. You shouldn't take things for granted. Perhaps after all the affinity between Matt and Dolly had been damaged by this stranger whom Hinton couldn't even remember coming across in the village. Perhaps prior claims would insist on their hold over Dolly.

Christmas came, in a spell of cold, frosty weather. In the farm kitchen after milking the family of Emmerdale exchanged their gifts. Annie had knitted sweaters for her menfolk. Sam had made a wooden letter holder for Joe's business papers, a genuine shepherd's crook for Matt, an old-fashioned salt box for his daughter. From Jack in Rome came wonderous Italian gifts: chocolates in tinfoil and filled with liqueurs, silk for his mother, a handmade leather briefcase for Joe, a note case for Matt and, for his grandfather, a specially bound volume of the typed-up notes from the tape-recordings made by Basil Ackroyd some months ago – the memoirs of exploits in World War One shared by Sam.

After the exclamations of delight and the pleasure of looking at new things, it seemed to Annie that a quietness fell on them all. She understood that for Matt the festive season had lost most of its sparkle, but even Joe seemed subdued.

He had of course said nothing to her of the invitation from Lesley to spend Christmas at Hawthorn. He wouldn't have mentioned it much anyway, because Hawthorn was a house which held unhappy memories for the Sugdens. But of course it was greatly changed now. The Gibsons, being rich brewers, had done restorations and alterations; all very tasteful and without harm to the appearance of the place, but it wasn't the Hawthorn Cottage that Joe had known nor that Matt had shared with Peggy. All-electric it was now, gleaming and sparkling inside.

He and Lesley had agreed they'd meet in the Woolpack for a drink in the late evening, after her dinner with her grandparents. Joe was beginning to think it was a long time till half-past nine.

The Woolpack closed promptly that midday, after having very few customers. Henry always maintained it would be a saving on light and heat not to open midday on Christmas Day but, as Amos said: 'What would Walter do? Besides, it's my duty to open. I have my duty, Mr Wilks.'

Annie's Christmas meal was scheduled for two o'clock but by the time all the trimmings had been fetched from the oven and Sam had sharpened the carving knife to his satisfaction, events had stretched out as they always did so that when Amos and Henry arrived they were in at the beginning of the meal. The big old kitchen table was a picture with its steaming dishes, its sauces and garnishes and jellies, the bottle of wine and the special-occasion glasses, gleaming like rubies in the centre.

'Well,' said Henry, sniffing. 'That goose smells a treat.'

'Sit down, sit down. I'm just going to carve,' urged Sam.

They had just taken their places when a car's engine was heard. It was unusual enough on this particular day – when most people would be indoors with their families – to make them all look up in attention. To their surprise, it didn't go past the lane end, but turned in at the lane and came nearer.

Joe sprang up. He looked out of the window. A saloon car was coming into the farmyard and parking alongside Henry's.

'Visitors!' he called.

Sam looked momentarily vexed. Annie glanced about to see that there was sherry to offer if it was by any chance Gladys Bullock or Tippy Scawbrook. Joe had opened the door.

On the threshold stood Lesley Gibson, with behind her two elderly persons with whom Joe was only slightly acquainted – her grandmother and grandfather.

'Hey-up!' he said. 'I didn't expect to see you.'

'Can we come in?' Lesley said.

'Come in,' called Annie. 'Merry Christmas!'

'Not so merry,' Lesley admitted with a rueful glance as she ushered in her grandparents. 'We've fused ourselves out of a Christmas dinner.'

'What!'

'Stove's gone kaput. Can't do a thing with it.'

'No!' Annie cried, bustling to make the newcomers welcome. 'What a nuisance. How did it happen?'

'No idea! Grannie's never been happy with it – have you, Grannie?'

'It's too complicated,' Mrs Gibson said. 'I'm used to electric but this one's really a bit much.'

'Did you get breakfast cooked?' Annie inquired.

'We didn't have much,' Mr Gibson said in a rather regretful tone. 'Looking forward to this tremendous turkey, y'know. Toast in the toaster, coffee in the percolator.'

'It was when Grannie came to switch on to start the turkey,' Lesley explained. 'It's a huge bird, going to take all day. But nothing would work.'

'I've had the back off to look at the works, and re-wired all the plugs,' Mr Gibson explained. 'Not a sausage!'

'Well, then, of course,' said Annie, 'you must stop and have Christmas dinner with us!'

Joe flashed a glance at Lesley and she smiled. He understood at once that it had been her suggestion to come to Emmerdale. They could have driven to Leeds for a meal at a hotel, but she had had a better idea. After all, wasn't it better to spend Christmas with neighbours rather than hotel acquaintances?

For Joe, at least, Christmas Day had got its sparkle back.

It would be true to say that everyone had a good time. Even Matt joined in the merrymaking – or at least enough to make it seem he was enjoying it. If his mother-in-law from time to time gave him an anxious scrutiny, no one else noticed.

Business was good in the Woolpack that evening and on Boxing Day. Amos was in high good humour, though he didn't let it show.

Then, when the postal service resumed, he got a letter that switched everything off as effectively as the fuse had put paid to Mrs Gibson's electric cooker.

'Dear Mr Brearley,' wrote Dolly, 'being at home with my mother has made me see I ought not to be so far from her. I am therefore writing to ask you to accept my notice, or at least to let me go, and keep the money due for my week's holiday as in lieu of notice. I'm sorry to do this so suddenly but I think it's best. There are a few of my things at the Woolpack and of course more at Emmerdale. I wonder if you'd be so good as to ask Mrs Sugden to pack up my belongings and send them to me, care of my mother (address above). I may not actually be here when the items arrive but Mother will take them in. Thank you for everything. Please give my regards to all kind friends in Beckindale.'

'Bye!' exclaimed Amos.

'What's up!'

'She's resigned, Mr Wilks! Miss Acaster has resigned her employment.'

'What?' shouted Wilks.

It was the worst news he could have heard. He'd been looking forward to Dolly's reurn. He was tired of tidying up and dusting, tired of hearing Amos complain of being overworked in the Christmas rush, tired of never having anything

129

decent to eat unless he went and cadged a meal at Emmer-dale.

'Young persons these days,' mourned Amos, 'they've no sense of responsibility.'

'What reason does she give?' Henry asked.

'She don't give a real reason.'

'You'd say, of course, that's she's decided to get wed to Richard Roper.'

'Nay,' said Amos. 'Not yet, any road.'

'Oh? How d'you know?'

Amos remembered the date he'd overheard them making as they came back into the Woolpack that night. January 4th. That was when they were to meet. On that day, pre-sumably, Dolly was going to give her answer to the man who claimed to be her fiancé.

'I have my thoughts on that subject,' he replied to his partner's query.

'Well, now you'd best give some thought to what we're going to do about a replacement.'

Amos let his shoulders droop a little. 'There's nobody suitable, and you know it.'

'Aye, and I've always known it. That's why I kept trying to make you treat Dolly a bit decent. It's no surprise to me she's packed up!'

'Miss Acaster always told me she wanted to learn the trade. Nobody ever learnt anything by being allowed to make mistakes.'

'Oh, Amos!' Henry cried. 'Do you know what's in front of us now? Months and months of scratch meals, of trying to take hold of the housework, of always making arrangements about who's to be in and who's to be out because we've no stand-in for the bar!'

'We managed,' Amos said. 'We'll manage again.'

But his lofty resolution was somewhat shaken when he sat down to the midday meal prepared by Henry, and found that the cook had forgotten to put salt in the potatoes but had put too much in the cabbage.

'Mr Wilks, that cabbage has nearly taken the roof off my mouth!'

'I'm sorry, Amos! I got called to the phone while I was doing it and must've put two lots in one saucepan instead of one lot in each.' Henry salted his potatoes. 'Dolly would never have done that,' he sighed.

A flicker of movement in the bar caught Amos's eye. 'Someone wants serving,' he observed.

'Well, it's your turn.'

'Nay, it's yours. I just served Walter and Bob Overton.'

'But I'm on duty in the kitchen – you're on duty in the bar.'

'Mr Wilks, we arranged we'd take it in turns to serve in t'bar at meal times.'

'Did we? I don't remember that. And meanwhile, Amos, somebody's waiting for his drink.'

Unable to resist the thought of an unserved customer, Amos got up and hurried into the bar.

During the afternoon Amos rang Emmerdale to tell Annie of Dolly's decision. 'Not coming back?' she repeated. 'Oh, Amos, I am sorry to hear that.'

'Well, that's as may be,' he said, in a rather haughty tone. 'She asked me to let you know and to say that she's got some stuff of hers at Emmerdale.'

'Yes, that's right.'

'She wants you to pack it up and send it on. To her Ma.'

'Is that where she is now?'

'Aye. But from what she says it seems she may not be staying there. Got another job lined up, I daresay.'

'I see.' She hesitated. 'When did you hear?'

'This morning.'

'Only I thought ... she might have written to Matt.'

'Mmm,' said Amos.

That day ended with an argument in the Woolpack about the bar takings. The shortage was only forty-eight pence, but Amos was very put out. 'You know as well as I do, Mr Wilks – there's a saying, "Take care of the pence and the pounds will take care of themselves."'

'It's quite clear. You gave somebody a fifty pence piece instead of a two pence.'

'I did? I never made a mistake in change in my life!'

131

'Well, I hardly took any money, all evening. You had me scurrying around picking up glasses and washing 'em.'

'Someone has to do it,' Amos pointed out.

'Dolly used to do it,' Henry said. '*And* keep the till straight.'

'It was no act of mine that made that cash short,' Amos declared.

'Well, it wasn't me.'

'How's it to be accounted for then?'

'Oh, for goodness sake, Amos, what does it matter?' Henry delved in his pocket, produced a handful of change, and held it towards his partner. 'Take it out of that.'

'That's not the way a business is run, Mr Wilks —'

'You mean you'd rather stand here glooming over forty-eight pence until tomorrow morning?' Henry demanded. 'I for one want to get to my bed.'

In the end Amos compromised by putting forty-eight pence of his own money in the till on the grounds that whoever had made a mistake, it was more likely to have been Mr Wilks but that it was beneath his dignity to accept the cash. He went up to bed at last in a melancholy frame of mind, not improved when he found he had stripped the sheets off to send them to the laundry earlier in the day and forgotten to put fresh on.

He woke next morning unrefreshed and ruffled after a night spent on a hastily made bed. He found Henry in the kitchen making an early morning cup of tea. 'I know where that forty-eight pence went short,' Henry said. 'It came to me last night. I forgot to put in the cash for a brandy I treated myself to. I'll give you the money later.'

Amos groaned.

'What's up? Headache?'

'No, Mr Wilks, I'm quite all right. A bit depressed, but that's neither here nor there.'

'A hot cup of tea will cheer you up,' said Henry. The kettle boiled. He warmed the teapot. He fetched the caddy.

The tea caddy was empty.

Neither man spoke. But each was thinking: Dolly would never have let us run out of tea.

Amos was forced to a decision. He was unwilling to admit to himself that he wanted Dolly back, but as the days went by the discomfort of life in the Woolpack without her became more and more obvious. Henry never missed a chance to rub it in: 'Dolly would have done this, Dolly would have seen to that.'

The final stroke was when Henry remarked: 'What I can't understand is why Matt doesn't take the bit between his teeth.'

'Matt?'

'Skilbeck. You remember him, Amos – played the First Shepherd in the play you reviewed for the *Courier*.'

This was another sore point. The *Courier* had cut Amos's glowing tribute to Beckindale's production to: 'A performance of the Yorkshire Shepherds Play was given in the Parish Church by the choir and inhabitants of Beckindale.' What made it worse was that Amos had told everyone to buy the *Courier* so as to read the essay of praise he had sent in.

'I don't see how Matt comes into it – about Miss Acaster, I mean.'

'Oh, come on, Amos. Even you must have known they were getting keen on each other.'

'Well ... I know they were friends ...'

'Bit more than that, I'd say.' Henry sighed. 'Too late now. She's gone – out of his reach.'

Amos gasped.

'What's the matter?'

'Nothing.'

'Indigestion? I *thought* that liver was a bit overcooked!'

'I've not got indigestion, Mr Wilks. Thank you.'

What he'd got was a great idea.

He appeared at Emmerdale during the afternoon. Annie had just come back from taking a flask of tea out to Joe and Matt. He hovered uncertainly in the doorway as she came in.

'Annie,' he said, 'I happen to be in possession of important information – and I don't know what to do with it.'

'Oh?' she said. 'Come in and have a cup of tea.'

With the tea came a piece of cheesecake. The difference between the fare offered here and at the Woolpack could hardly have been more marked. It spurred him on. 'Annie, I know where Dolly Acaster will be this evening!'

She turned from the task of pouring him a second cup. 'You do?'

'I ... er ... couldn't help overhearing the two of 'em –'

'What two?'

'Her and this Roper chap. They were coming in after a private chat. He said to her, "That's a date then – The Red Lion on the fourth of January" or summat like that.'

'I see.'

'What should I do, Annie?'

'About what?'

'Well, *you* know.'

'No, I don't, Amos.'

He was astounded that she could be so obtuse. 'About telling Matt.'

'Matt?'

'Well, I mean, it's well known. Him and Dolly ... Until this chap Roper came along ... I mean, since she's been gone, Matt's been really down, hasn't he?'

'Amos!' Annie said, staring at him. She was completely taken aback. It had never crossed her mind that Amos would care one way or the other about Matt's affairs. But Amos had a sense of indebtedness to the Sugden family: without their help over the Butterworth Ball, what would have become of him?

'So will you tell him, Annie, or shall I?' he asked.

The thought of Amos trying to convey delicate information to Matt was too much to bear. 'I'll tell him,' she said hastily.

'Good.' Amos looked relieved. 'It'll come better from you. No need to tell him how you came by the information, eh?'

'All right, Amos. And ... thank you.'

She got rid of her father by asking Joe to take him to the Woolpack for a drink after tea. Matt sat down with the newspaper by the fire. She said: 'Matt, I know where Dolly is.'

Matt looked up, then returned to his paper. 'With her Ma, you mean.'

'No. She's at the Red Lion in Brassington.'

He kept his gaze on the newsprint. 'Brassington?'

'Yes. She's meeting that Mr Roper there.'

Now he folded the paper and gave her his full attention. 'Meeting him?'

'Aye.'

'What for?'

'To try to sort things out, happen.'

He nodded. 'They've got things to sort out, those two. They meant a lot to each other once.'

'Because of the baby, you mean?'

'Yes.'

'That's true enough. But there's more than that. He uses it as a hold over her, Matt.'

'A hold?'

'He can ... have the baby found. Wreck its peaceful little life.'

'Nay,' Matt said, getting up. 'Nobody'd do that –'

'Are you sure? Think of the man we saw – I'm not sure he would hold back, if it was something he wanted. And that's why Dolly can't say no if he asks to meet her.'

'Annie!'

She came to him and sat down in the chair across the hearth. Her gaze was full on him, steady and serious. 'You love her, lad.' It was a statement, not a question.

He had never been one to talk about emotions. He didn't know what to say. 'Well ... I ... We never actually said ...'

'And she loves you.'

'How can you be sure?'

'Oh, Matt,' she said, gently. 'She loves you. She does.'

He gave a half-nod. 'I felt that ... happen ... she might...'

'Why don't you just ask each other how you feel?'

'But she's meeting *him*.'

'At a hotel. Anyone can go in.'

He stared at her. 'You're suggesting I should just ... turn up?'

135

'Well, I don't think he should have things all his own way, do you? And Dolly's fighting with one hand tied behind her back.'

'But she ... she's never asked for help ...'

'And since when have you waited to be asked, lad? Anybody else but Dolly, you'd have leapt to her defence.'

He set the newspaper aside. He got up. 'I think I'll just go up and change into my suit,' he said.

About half an hour later Matt Skilbeck, dressed for town, walked into the Woolpack. Joe and Sam hailed him, but he merely nodded and waved. He went to the bar. Amos looked at him with some apprehension.

'Amos, would you cash a cheque for me?'

Henry was nearby, drying glasses. 'Oh, Matt, don't ask a question like that. "Do not ask for credit as a refusal gives offence".'

'How much would you like?' asked Amos, with the till already open.

'Eh?' gasped Henry.

'Could you manage ten?' Matt offered a cheque.

'Sure that's enough?'

'I hope so. I just want a bit of cash on me. I've got my cheque book for owt else.'

Before Henry's amazed glance Amos accepted the cheque, put it under the clip where the notes were kept, and waved farewell to Matt. Matt nodded and hurried out. Joe and Sam, half rising to speak to him, sat back in surprise.

'Amos!' breathed Henry, taking him by the arm and pulling him away from the cash register. 'Are you all right?'

'Quite all right, ta.'

'But ... but ... you've never cashed a cheque for anybody in your life before!'

'Well, a man needs a bit of money on him when he's going to see his girl.'

'What? Who –? Matt? You mean Matt's going to see Dolly?'

'Could be.'

'Good Lord.'

136

'Besides, if he brings her back, we won't have to do any more cleaning and cooking.'

Henry leaned on the bar and drew in a breath. 'Ee-hh, Amos!' he sighed.

CHAPTER TEN

When Richard Roper arrived at the Red Lion in Brassington, he found that the name immediately above his in the register was that of Miss D. Acaster.

He was surprised. He didn't think she'd get here first, he didn't think she'd take a room and stay overnight. He didn't think she'd come at all. He'd been half prepared for a long, fruitless wait, stoking his anger against her.

But she was here already.

When he'd unpacked he put through a call to her room.

'Oh – Richard? Yes, I got here this morning.' It was a shock to her to hear his voice. She was very nervous, tense with dread.

'Shall we meet for a drink in the bar, and then have dinner?'

'If you like.'

When she came down she was wearing a sweater dress with a high roll collar. From it her face emerged looking vulnerable, fragile. She hadn't done it on purpose to look appealing. She felt the cold these days – never seemed to be able to get warm. The coming interview with Richard had chilled her to the bone.

They settled with their drinks in the lounge, a chintzy place half empty now that Christmas had come and gone. There was a big log fire in a granite fireplace. She could hear the hissing of the sap in the logs.

'Thank you for coming,' he said.

'I promised I would.'

'But I didn't really believe ...'

She sipped her Martini. He didn't know her, never had known her, if he really thought she wouldn't keep a promise.

To his own surprise, he was at a loss. He'd been so sure she wouldn't come, or would be late. He would have been ready with angry words on that score.

'How did the wedding go?' she inquired with politeness. 'The one in Perth?'

'Oh, well ... You know. The mother of the bride cried, the best man made an embarrassed speech, everybody drank too much.'

She looked up, smiling almost with mischief. 'At least you were spared that, Richard!'

'You mean, because you and I never ...? I wish we had, Dolly.'

'Too late.'

'No it isn't! I still feel the same about you –'

'The same? How? The way you felt when we were together, or the way you felt when you wouldn't come to England after hearing about the baby?'

'Dolly!'

'Well, how? I mean, let's be truthful with each other. If we aren't, there's no point in being here talking to each other.'

'You've got to understand that I never stopped loving you, Dolly! It was just that when you tried to force my hand by leaving me, I was hurt and angry. And so I let myself be dragged off to Durban. All right, I should have come back – I realise that now. But I let myself be over-persuaded. That's finished. I've done a lot of growing up since then.'

She shook her head.

'I have, Dolly!'

'It's not very grown up to arrive out of nowhere after nearly three years and expect me to fall into your arms. It's not very grown up to get angry and sulky –'

'Sulky!'

'Sulky, when I refuse to agree with your view of things. It's not very grown up to threaten other people's lives just because you can't make your own go the way you want it.'

'I haven't threatened anybody.'

'The baby?' she said at once. 'Our baby? You're threatening to break up his life.'

'There's no threat in that. I could do so much more for him.'

'How do you know? How do you know what parents he's got now? He might be with millionaires for all we know.' She put down her glass with clumsy haste. 'Richard – you haven't found him?'

'No . . . But I will.'

'Don't do it.'

'But he's my son, Dolly.'

'No. He's not even my son. He belongs to the people who adopted him, who've had him since he was three weeks old. They've made his bottles for him and changed his nappies and seen him through the miseries of his first tooth. He's *their* son.'

'But I was never even asked if I wanted him given away to strangers.'

'Your mother spoke for you. She couldn't wait to see him safely out of the way.'

'So you say. I've no proof my mother went along with the idea. I've got a good case in law, as the natural father who was never consulted.'

'You mean you'd tell lies, Richard? Pretend you didn't know how your mother handled it?' Dolly sighed. 'Didn't you just tell me you'd done a lot of growing up? I thought adults knew the difference between truth and lies.'

He shook the ice around in his glass so that it tinkled. 'You think faster than you used to,' he admitted. 'I used to be able to get you in a right old muddle when it came to an argument.'

'But then,' she said, in a weary voice, 'I've done a lot of growing up too, you see.'

He drank off his gin and got up. 'Come on, let's eat. All this dissension is caused by talking on an empty stomach.'

During the meal he insisted on talking trivialities. Perhaps it was as well, for the waiters kept hovering round. In an empty hotel, they wanted to exercise their talents on what few guests they had. Richard asked for coffee in the lounge. When they had settled themselves in a comfortable sofa, he stretched out his legs and clasped his hands behind his head.

'Not a bad place, this. We'll come here often, I expect.'

'No.'

'Why not? Nice part of the country. A bit cold in winter, but I daresay there's good shooting. And in summer, it might be very pleasant.'

'I'm trying for a job in Lytham St Anne's.'

'Don't be absurd, Dolly! You'll be marrying me quite soon.'

'I won't, Richard. Put that out of your head. No matter what you do – about the boy, I mean – I'll never marry you.'

They could see the elderly waiter approaching with the silver tray of coffee. Neither spoke except in answer to his queries. 'Black or white, madam? Sir? Sugar? Mints in the dish, sir. Thank you, sir. Anything else?'

Richard shook his head. He'd wanted a brandy but now he couldn't bear another interruption. He wanted to snare Dolly once and for all.

She left it to him to take up the word. He began from a different angle. 'You're leaving your job at that funny old pub?'

'I've left it already.'

'Really? I thought you'd just come from there.'

'No, I spent Christmas with my mother in Darlington.'

'Dear girl, how dire! I was imagining you with those nice people at ... where was it ... Emmerdale.'

'No.'

'How are they, do you know? How is your friend Matt?'

'I've no idea.'

'A complete break, is that it?'

'It seemed best.'

'Why?' he flashed. 'Because they're so narrowminded they'd never let you forget your past now they've learned it?'

'Oh, Richard,' she sighed. 'Don't you realise how utterly

wrong you are? It's just the opposite. You're bringing with you nothing but unrest and . . . and pain. Because they're such good friends, they'd feel they had to intervene. And then they'd get hurt. I don't want that.'

'So you agreed to come and be with me here so as to keep Matt from getting hurt.'

'I agreed to come and talk to you, yes.'

'Oh, come on. The two of us in the same hotel overnight? Don't be naive.'

'Don't you be naive!' she said, suddenly sharp, taking him by surprise. 'A man that strides about in my life telling folk he's going to marry me! A man who threatens children! D'you really think I'm going to melt into your arms?'

'Methinks the lady doth protest too much –'

'Methinks the lady will lock her door tonight, and don't think I won't ring down to the night porter if you rattle the handle, Richard!'

'You're being a bit harpy-ish, aren't you?'

'Oh, there's steel in me, Richard. You just never saw it while we were living together. Because I kept giving in then, you think I'll give in again. But I want you to understand this, lad.' She pounded her fist softly against the tapestry of the sofa arm as she spoke, 'Nothing you do – *nothing* – will make me take up with you again.'

'I think I could find ways to make you change your mind.'

'You think I'll cave in? Try me.'

'What if I say I'll drop the inquiry to find our little boy?'

She shook her head. 'No.'

'You mean you wouldn't care if I went on with that?'

'Oh, I'd care. I'd break my heart. But you'd break yours, and his, and everybody else's.' She took hold of the sleeve of his dinner jacket. 'Go on. Spend six months, a year, finding him. Go through all the legal complications. You can't have him, Richard. They won't let you have him. He's legally adopted. And it will count against you that you tracked him down, were callous enough to destroy his new life, just so as to get him for yourself – I was going to say, get him back, but he was never yours! Never.'

'If I had a good lawyer to speak for me –'

'Oh, lawyers! They talk to each other, they don't talk to ordinary folk. Do you know what people call someone who destroys the lives of innocent children? Herod!'

She threw the name at him. From his childhood there came back the words from the lessons in church: 'For Herod will seek the young child to destroy him.' Despite himself, he felt a shiver of revulsion.

'I only want what's good for him, Dolly –'

'Then leave him alone! What he needs is security, peace, an ordinary life! If you take that away, you're harming him. Even if you didn't win your case to have him awarded to you, you'd have caused anxiety, misery, to his parents. He'd know, he'd feel it. How do you think he'd feel when he was handed to you, if it ever happened? I can just hear him – "Thank you, real Daddy, for dragging me away from everybody who's ever cared for me!"'

'Well, I've told you – I would be prepared to let that go,' he countered. 'If you and I –'

'And I've told you, it's never going to happen.' She took a grip on herself, and spoke in a very quiet, restrained tone. 'I don't love you, Richard. I did once, but that's gone. You've changed, I've changed, we're not the same people any more.'

'But we could start again, darling –'

'I don't want to. Why don't you understand? I don't want to. There was something I wanted . . . hoped for . . . but you've put paid to all that. Barging about in my life, showing off, making wild threats against a little boy . . . Do you think I could love a man like that?'

'But Dolly, I didn't mean any of that. Not really. I was just so . . . at a loss, when you refused even to listen to me. I was really only trying to make you pay me some heed.'

'Oh, I did that. You succeeded marvellously. I looked at you, Richard.' She shook her head. 'And I didn't like what I saw.'

'That's unfair –'

'It's true. I don't even like you. If we had met now, as strangers, I don't think I'd have bothered to exchange more

142

than ten words with you.'

She had made him angry. He said in a hard voice: 'So you say now. But that wasn't how it was three years ago, was it? Couldn't wait, could you? And how you went off me when you discovered there were to be no wedding bells!'

'I was a scheming little cat, wasn't I?'

'Too true! My mother warned me from the off –'

'Yes. I know she did. And now you see she was right, is that it?'

'Well, I –'

'You see?' Dolly said, sad and quiet now. 'You don't think about a person you love like that. You're not really in love with me, lad.'

'But I am! I've come all this way to find you again, to have you with me and to get our son –'

'Nay, you're lonely. That's what it is. You're on your own and lost without your mother, and you remembered the good times we had, and how you could blame our parting on me or your mother, and take up with me as if nothing had been your fault. You'd have someone to turn to again, someone to help you fill in your time. I understand, Richard.' She nodded gently. 'I know what it is to be lonely. But I can't help you.'

'You think you're so clever!' he cried. 'You don't understand a bit. I've lived and dreamed for the moment when we could be together again. I was going to build my life around the two of us – the three of us –'

'You'll have to find someone else, love. I'm not on for the job.'

'But it could work, Dolly! We used to be such friends – as well as being in love.'

'That's true. But ... well ... sometimes we grow out of friendships, you know. I had friends at school – "best friends" – I never see them now. But more than that, I would always remember the things you said about the little lad – the way you were ready to use him like a weapon. I don't want to say it just to hurt you, Richard. But I can't be friends with a man who'd say things like that.'

Richard sighed and stared down at his clasped hands. 'What

143

goes wrong?' he said, almost as if to himself. 'Why do we say and do things that spoil everything? I didn't mean it. I never really meant it.'

'You see, now, don't you, that you have to leave the boy alone?'

'Oh yes. Of course.'

'You won't put detectives on to him?'

'No.'

'Thank God for that.'

'You think better of me for that?' He looked up.

'I always think better of good men than of bad, Richard. And there is good in you, I know.' Relief was flooding through her. Some sixth sense told her that the fever, the delirium, had left him. At last he accepted the facts – that there could never be anything more between the two of them and that the baby he had never seen was gone from both their lives.

She truly believed he'd been as if under a delusion until now. He had persuaded himself that he could put the clock back. He had shut out reality, convinced he would make everyone else act as he felt they ought to act.

When she had refused to play her role, he had only tried the harder to preserve his own fantasy. Something like hysteria had possessed him. A climax had to come before the fever would break. Dolly had been uncertain if she could bring it about, if she had the nerve or the skill. But she was the only person to make the attempt and so she had come to this encounter. She'd been prepared for almost anything – argument, abuse, perhaps even some cruel trick to put her in the wrong. She had expected defeat.

And now here he sat, his shoulders drooping, the fight gone out of him. He looked drawn and tired – older.

'Let's have some more coffee,' she suggested. She beckoned the waiter and when he came, gave her order. Richard asked for a double brandy.

'What will you do now?' she asked.

'I don't know. Go home, I suppose.'

'To Durban?'

'Yes.'

'You've friends there,' she said in encouragement.

'Of course. Just as you have here.' He paused. 'Will you really go to Lytham wherever?'

'Yes. I've hopes of a job there.'

'It's no kind of a life, Dolly – moving about from one place to another, always in someone else's home, at someone else's beck and call.'

'Oh, well,' she said brightly, 'there are prospects. Some day I might run a place of my own.'

'If it's money –'

'No, Richard.'

'No, of course not. What about settling down? I mean, a pub usually has a man about the place.'

'I'm not giving that any thought.'

The waiter brought fresh coffee and the brandy. Richard swallowed some thankfully; she could see he really needed it, to revitalise him after the shock he'd had at seeing his dream castle coming to pieces.

'What about him?' he said after a moment.

'Who?'

'Oh, you know well enough. Matt.'

'That's all over.'

'My fault?'

'Happen I'm to blame too. I let you put me in a flurry. But when last comes to last . . . he'd never asked me, Richard.'

Richard smiled at her waveringly. 'He must be a fool,' he said.

'I don't think so. He's just not reached the point of knowing how he really felt – and the way things happened, he never got the chance. He lost his bearings. Any road, happen he'd have decided against it,' she said, trying to sound brisk. 'He'd been married already, you know.'

'Good God,' Richard said cruelly, 'don't tell me he'd been divorced!'

'Oh no! His wife died. It was very tragic. And he lost his family – twins. I don't know the whole story, he doesn't talk about it. But he's known tragedy.' She studied Richard over the tiny coffee cup. 'I don't want to nag on at you, Richard, but you don't know what you're doing when you rush in like that. You see a peaceful valley with quiet folk in it, and you think: "Never known a bit of trouble in their lives. Slow as snails, they are." But it's not so. Matt's known suffering. And happen that's why he doesn't rush after a glimpse of happiness – he needs to know it isn't a will-o'-the-wisp.'

Richard was looking past her towards the arch that gave access to the hall. 'I think a particular will-o'-the-wisp has led him in the right direction tonight,' he remarked.

'What?'

'He's here. Looking for you, I imagine.'

She turned, and saw him. He was inside the arch, his eyes moving among the chairs and settees. Dolly and Richard, deep in their sofa, weren't easy to see.

Dolly got up, trying to set her cup on the low table and missing it. She was quite unaware of the falling cup and saucer.

She hurried towards him. Matt put out his hands.

She put hers into his. He pulled her towards him so that her head rested against his shoulder.

'I was worried about you,' he said.

'Oh, Matt! I never expected to see you here!'

'Are you all right?'

'I'm fine. Fine! Specially now you're here!'

'I should have come for you at your mother's,' he said, 'when Amos got that letter. Only I wasn't sure ...'

'What?'

'Whether he'd be there with you.'

'Oh no,' she said. And then with a shaky laugh, 'Oh no! My mother wouldn't let him in the house!'

Matt recalled little things Dolly had let slip about her mother and realised that Mrs Acaster had always disapproved of Richard. If Dolly's mother had stood by her when the baby was born, happen Dolly wouldn't have had to let it be adopted. He saw now, as he ought to have seen if he'd been thinking clearly, that while Dolly was staying with her mother the last person to visit her there was Richard Roper.

'Come and sit down,' Dolly urged. They turned, without parting from each other, Matt's arm still around her shoulder. They moved towards the sofa.

Watching them come, Richard was filled with a seething resentment. Why should *he* be so quick to comfort her? Why should she accept from *him* what she wouldn't accept from Richard?

Richard didn't get up. He lounged back in the sofa. 'Good evening. I didn't expect you?'

'I didn't expect me myself,' Matt said with easy good nature. He felt no animosity towards Richard, suddenly. He understood at last that Richard was nothing to be afraid of.

Dolly and Richard had been sitting together on the deep sofa. Richard now patted the place for Dolly, but made no movement of invitation towards Matt. He wanted to show that Matt was an intruder, wanted to put him off balance.

But Matt was too straightforward to be flummoxed by clever one-upmanship. He beckoned a waiter. 'Bring us a chair up, lad,' he requested.

'Two chairs,' said Dolly.

And when they were brought, she and Matt sat alongside each other, on armless fireside chairs, while Richard remained in solitary splendour on the sofa.

'I suppose you haven't had dinner?' Richard said. 'I don't know if they're still serving, but I expect they could knock up a meal for you –'

'No thanks,' said Matt. 'I had my tea at five-thirty.'

Richard smiled. Tea at five-thirty. He glanced at Dolly to see if she understood his amusement at the notion. But she was looking with some concern at Matt.

'You've had a long drive. You'll have something. A drink? Coffee?'

'A pint would go down all right.'

'That's it, then.' She caught the eye of the waiter who was hovering, expecting an order. Richard asked for another brandy. He knew he was drinking too much, but he felt in need of solace.

'To what do we owe this pleasure?' he inquired.

147

'I got worried about Dolly.'

'There was no need,' Richard said with acidity. 'I assure you Dolly is well able to take care of herself.'

'Oh?' Matt said, with a glance at her.

'Yes, everything's all right, Matt. But I'm right glad to see thee.'

'How did you know where we were?' Richard inquired.

'Dunno. It sort of ... became known. Why? Was it a secret?'

Richard darted a furious look at him. How was it that this man could keep putting him wrong-footed?

'We certainly had confidential matters to discuss,' he told him, very chill.

'But we'd finished, Richard –'

'And any road I could always go and have my pint in t'bar, if you want to chat on for a bit.'

'Chat on for a bit?' echoed Richard, staggered.

'Nay, it's not necessary. You and I had settled everything.'

Luckily at that moment the waiter came with the drinks, causing a welcome diversion for Richard. Afterwards he started from another tack.

'How's your mother – no, mother-in-law, isn't it?'

'She's fine. She hasn't packed up your things yet, Dolly. Happen she won't have to bother now.'

'No, that's right.'

'How did the Nativity Play go? Did you manage to get through your part without drying up?' inquired Richard.

'It went well,' Matt said, side-stepping the implied insult. 'Amos wrote what I think's called a "rave review" but t'*Courier* never printed it.' He drank some of his pint. 'My, that's not bad. Amos ought to inquire who supplies the Red Lion. By t'way, Dolly, Mr Hinton is anxious to thank you for the costumes and that.'

'Oh ... that's kind. I didn't do anything.'

'You're mistaken, Dolly. Clearly you've turned into a pillar of Beckindale society. Rather unexpected, considering your former life, eh?'

Matt stiffened, and Dolly felt an inward shiver. He was

determined to have a quarrel; Richard wasn't a man who could just slacken his grasp and let something go.

'Y'know,' Matt said, 'I don't know what t'world's like in South Africa, but round here folks are much the same where-ever you look. Most families are a mixture of the settled-down kind and the adventurous. Us at Emmerdale — we've got a lad who went out and ... well, the old saying was he sowed his wild oats. A lot has happened to Jack. But that don't mean we think the less of him.'

'Jack? Did I meet him?'

'No, he lives in Rome. Does his writing there.'

'Jack? Sugden? Jack Sugden, the novelist?'

'Well, aye, I suppose that's what you'd call him. To us, he's our Jack.'

Richard sat staring at him, utterly baulked. He had read Jack's bestselling novel, with its frank portrayal of what had clearly been the author's own life. He had seen items in the newspapers about Jack: winning a prize for the best film script, having some sort of affair with a married Italian actress ...

It came to Richard, with the certainty of defeat, that it was useless to speak to Matt Skilbeck of the wickedness of Dolly's past. Dolly's past would be accepted and set aside, just as Jack Sugden's was.

It just showed, didn't it ... Dolly was right when she said quiet folk weren't necessarily shallow folk.

Perhaps it was this conclusion, or perhaps it was the somnolence brought on by too many brandies, but Richard almost gave up the fight from then on. He chatted about Jack Sugden, who genuinely interested him. The time went by. All of a sudden Matt was stifling a yawn.

Dolly caught him at it. 'Tired?'

'Not really,' he said, as if giving himself a little shake. He looked at his watch. 'Ten-thirty. I'm usually off to bed by now.'

'At this hour?' Richard cried.

'Well — milking's five-thirty, you see.'

'Good lord.'

'It's wrong to keep you like this, Matt,' Dolly said. 'What about getting back?'

'D'you want to go?' Matt said.

Richard came to life again. 'Dolly's staying overnight.'

'I've a room booked,' Dolly put in quickly.

'So have I,' said Matt.

Dolly gazed at him in surprise and admiration. Richard was silenced. Then he recovered. 'In that case, don't let's stop you if you want to pop up to bye-byes.'

'I think I can prop my eyelids up a bit longer.'

'Acting chaperon, are you?'

'Never thought of that. Do you feel you need one?'

Richard got up. 'I think I'll find the night porter and get another drink. You?'

'No thanks, I've had all I need.'

'Dolly?'

'No thanks.'

'Am I going to drink alone? Never let it be said!'

'All right then,' she said hastily, to keep his voice from rising further. 'I'll have another sherry.'

'Right you are.' He stalked off. He was furious. He felt the whole thing had slipped away from him. Perhaps if he had a minute by himself to think, he might come up with something.

Matt watched him go. 'Couldn't he have rung t'bell?'

'Oh yes. But ... I think he needs to get away for a minute. He's been suffering. You could see that.'

'Suffering?'

'I mean, feeling bad. He's not used to coming second.'

Matt grinned and took her hand. 'I know how he feels. I'm like that, t'other way round. I can't quite come to terms wi' it.'

'Oh, Matt ...'

'I came because ... I thought you might need a helping hand.'

'Aye.'

'But he seems kind of subdued.'

'He's come to a sort of watershed. It shook him, I think.'

'Oh, but when he were in t'village, before Christmas ... he seemed to have the upper hand all the time.'

'That was my fault. I should have fought back.'

'He told Amos you were going to marry him.'

'He told *me* I was going to marry him!'

'But you're not.'

She squeezed his hand. 'Don't be daft.'

'Sorry.'

'Here comes my drink.' She detached his grasp, and accepted the sherry from Richard. The fact that her hand had been in Matt's wasn't lost on Richard.

'I brought you another pint,' he said to Matt.

'Good of you, but I've finished for tonight.'

'Oh, go on, man. What's the matter? Can't hold your drink?'

'Never pushed it to a limit where I had to find out.'

Richard sat down, tossed off his brandy, and laughed. 'That's the difference between you and me. I like to go the limit.'

'Aye,' said Matt. It was the most unkind thing he'd said so far.

'What are you doing here, Matt?' Richard said in a tone of belligerence.

'What are you?'

'Trying to sort things out with Dolly.'

'Same here.'

'My word, Dolly, aren't you sought after!'

Dolly had put her sherry on the coffee table, untouched. She now got up. 'I think I'll go up to bed,' she said.

Richard turned to Matt. 'It's all right, we've got separate rooms. We've done all the sharing bit. You didn't know that, did you?'

'Richard, you're getting too –'

'Too frank, is that it? But Matt ought to be in the picture, oughtn't he? He's made a long drive so it must be important. So he ought to be clued up.' He turned suddenly on Matt. 'Have *you*? Shared a bedroom with her?'

'Richard!' gasped Dolly.

Matt shook his head with some weariness. 'It's all right, love, don't thee fret.' To Richard he said: 'No, Mr Roper, Dolly and I haven't slept together. I dunno why it should bother you to know. I dunno what you'll make of the answer. But that's how it is. We're friends. Real friends. Happen you don't think that's much ...'

Richard pressed his lips together. After a moment he said uncertainly: 'No, I know it's a lot.'

'You asked me what I'm doing here,' Matt went on, very calm and steady. 'I'm here to tell Dolly she's wanted – she's needed – in Beckindale. I want her to come back to the farm with me, back to her friends, to her ... family.'

The other man gave a half-frown and seemed almost to flinch. He looked at Dolly.

Matt said: 'Will you come, Dolly?'

'Yes, Matt. I will.'

Richard shook his head. 'Is that all you have to say to him? After what must have been the longest speech he's ever made in his life – apart from the Nativity Play?'

'It's all I need to say, Richard.'

'Aye, and she didn't even have to say it. I knew.' Matt got up. 'Well, I'm for bed. See you in the morning. Goodnight, Mr Roper.'

'Goodnight.'

'Night, Dolly. See you at breakfast.'

'They don't serve breakfast at five-thirty,' Richard said, trying for lightness.

'Oh, I saw a Teamaker in my room,' Matt replied, equally light. He nodded to them both and went out.

After a long, baffled pause Richard said: 'And he can walk away and leave us together?'

Dolly smiled. 'You'll never understand, Richard.'

'Dammit, where did I go wrong? I ought to have run rings round him.'

'But he wasn't in a competition, lad. That's the difference. You've got this daft notion that everybody has to play by your rules. Matt's never even heard of them.'

Richard sighed. He felt sad. His head ached. He studied

152

Dolly. He couldn't even feel angry with her any more, though she looked happy and secure.

'So ...' he said. 'You may have other children.'

She answered the question he hadn't put into words. 'I won't forget ours,' she said. 'But he's all right, Richard. I know he is.'

He nodded. 'I just wish ...'

'Never mind, love. It's at an end.'

Next morning force of habit brought Matt awake by just after five-thirty. He made tea in his room, as he would have done at Emmerdale in the kitchen, and went out into the cold January morning. A few minutes' walk brought him to the edge of Brassington, and then there were the moors, stretching out into the darkness, breathing like a great quiet creature. Matt walked for an hour, letting his mind roam over what had happened last night and making indefinite plans for this morning.

Breakfast began at the hotel at seven-thirty. Matt was alone in the diningroom at first and had all the attention of all the waiters. He didn't mind. They were all leaping at him with fresh toast and offers of another grilled tomato. He got fresh tea without asking for it when he'd finished the first pot.

Dolly joined him at eight. He sat with her while she had breakfast. Not until nine did Richard appear.

'Hello,' he said. 'Have I kept you?'

'No hurry,' Matt said. 'I rang home to say where I was and what I was doing.'

'And what are you doing?'

'Waiting to say goodbye, and all that.'

'What about you, Dolly?'

'I'm waiting to say goodbye too.'

'You're going back with him now?'

'After breakfast.'

Richard ordered coffee and toast. He had a thick head. The idea of eating a cooked breakfast made him ill. 'Funny,' he said. 'In all the things I've imagined, I never thought I'd be sitting across a breakfast table from you, Matt.'

153

'Me neither.' Matt nodded at him. 'And there's no need to go on about who else you've seen at breakfast.'

'I wasn't going to.' Richard stirred his coffee. 'I know when I'm beaten.'

'I thought of heading for home. In about half an hour, Dolly.'

'All right, Matt.'

Matt and Dolly rose, to go upstairs and pack overnight bags. When Richard came out to the courtyard of the inn, he found the Land-Rover drawn up at the porch.

'You paid Dolly's bill?' he challenged.

'Aye. I thought it best.'

Richard had been going to make an issue of it. But all at once it seemed pointless. Of course, he understood. Dolly must owe him nothing when Matt drove her away.

Dolly got into the Land-Rover. 'Goodbye, Richard,' she said.

'Dolly –'

'Yes?'

'Don't think badly of me.'

'No, love. I promise.'

I promise, he thought, not to think badly of you. She won't think of me at all.

'Goodbye, Matt,' he said.

'Goodbye.' Matt hesitated and added: 'Good luck.'

'Yes. Thanks. I'm the one who's going to need it.'

'Richard,' Matt said unexpectedly, 'you've had good things in your life. Think about them, not about the bad things.'

Richard was going to say, 'It's easy for you.' Then he recalled what Dolly had told him of Matt's life. He stood back, raising a hand in farewell as the Land-Rover moved off.

In a way Dolly half-expected something to happen to make them turn around and go back. It seemed incredible that Richard couldn't stop her. But as the miles slipped away her confidence grew. She began to realise she was free. Really free.

'He could have been a feller I might have liked,' Matt remarked, 'if I'd met him some other way.'

154

'Aye. Poor Richard. He just ... tries too hard.'

'Aye.'

After another pause Matt began again. 'I know it's too soon to be saying it, happen. You've been upset, Richard put you in a right state. You need time, I s'pose. But ... I sort of have to say it.'

'What, Matt?'

'When you've got over all this ... You see, I think you need somebody to look after you. Don't you think it would be better?'

'What would?'

'If we got married.'

She took so long about replying that he glanced at her with alarm. Had he blundered? Was it far too soon?

'Please stop, Matt,' she said at last.

'Stop?'

'The Land-Rover. Can we stop a minute?'

'Oh ... aye ... of course.' He pulled in a a lay-by, switched off. 'You feeling all right?'

'What?'

'Not travel-sick, are you?'

She began to laugh. She put her hands up to her face and laughed in delight. After a moment, Matt began to laugh too. 'But you see,' he managed to say, 'when you told me to stop ...'

'It was for this, Matt.'

She slipped her arms round his neck.

'I really love you, Matt,' she said.

In response he put his arm about her. 'Well,' he said. 'Good.'

As they came into Beckindale it was about time for the mid-day meal. Amos had served Walter and having nothing else to do, had come out for a moment to breath the cold dry air. He saw the Land-Rover coming up the village street. Holding his breath, he watched.

Next to Matt in the front he could see Dolly.

'Well,' he said to himself with satisfaction, 'I'll tell Mr Wilks we can have a hot meal this evening ...'

155

The vicar was crossing to the post office as the Land-Rover came by. He waved to it to slow down. 'Miss Acaster!' he exclaimed. 'I'm so glad to see you! I wanted to tell you how wonderfully you helped me with the play.'

'Thank you, vicar. I'm glad the costumes worked.'

'Oh, everything worked. Splendid, really splendid.' He glanced at Matt. There was something about these two ... 'Everything all right, Matt?'

'Couldn't be better, Mr Hinton.'

'Really! I'm so glad.' He backed away to let them drive on. Prayers *are* answered, he said to himself.

At Emmerdale the meal was on the table. Sam was saying: 'Didn't he say if he was bringing her back?'

'I don't think he knew for sure at that moment.'

'I just don't know ...! Young folks these days! The pair of them, in the same hotel ... What'll folk think?'

'Nowt, Grandad,' Joe said. 'Who's going to tell them?'

'Oh, it'll get about. These things allus do.'

'I don't think so,' Annie remarked. 'We're the only ones that know – except for one other person.'

'What other person?' Sam was alarmed. 'Who? Who knows?'

Annie was spared the necessity of keeping Amos's name out of it by the arrival of the Land-Rover. Everyone leapt up and came pouring out. When Dolly stepped down, the equivalent of a cheer went up.

'Eeh, lass!' Same cried. 'We've been that worried about thee!'

'Have you? I'm sorry. Everything's all right, though.'

'Come in, you're just in time for dinner,' Annie said, ushering her in.

'I'll just take my case up ... If that's all right?'

'You'll find a clean towel on the chair,' Annie said, thus signalling that her room was ready for her.

'Oh, thank you, Mrs Sugden.' Dolly cast a glance about her. 'Oh, I have missed it all!'

She went upstairs with her bag. Matt followed, to drop his own in his room.

'I don't think you have to bother about the family's good name, Grandad,' Joe remarked as they sat down again at table. 'I think you could say they're engaged.'

'Humph,' said Sam. 'About time.'

Slowly, and with a few hitches, the day began to take its normal course. Matt changed into his work clothes and went out to continue with the lambing pens. Sam got potatoes out of the clamp for Annie. Annie embarked on a special cake for tonight's tea. Dolly went to the Woolpack.

Finding no one about, she took off her jacket and put on her pinny. When Henry came up from the cellar, he found her washing the remains of the dirty glasses from the lunch-time opening.

'Dolly!'

'Hello, Mr Wilks. Can I have my old job back?'

'Dolly! You never lost it, as far as I was concerned!'

'Thank you. T'place wants a duster over it, I see.'

'More than that! Oh, lass, I'm that glad to see you!'

'Where's Mr Brearley?'

'Out on a "story" for the *Courier*. Wait till he sees you.' Then Henry paused. 'And yet ... happen he's seen you already. When I asked him how he wanted that steak grilled for tonight, he told me not to worry about it because he thought it would be taken care of.'

'You think he's going to be all right about me coming back?'

'He'd better be. I'll shoot him otherwise.'

'Oh, Mr Wilks,' Dolly said, blinking back tears.

She worked away, catching up with all the chores. About half-past four, when the lights had been switched on and the Woolpack's interior was sparkling again, Matt looked in. 'Hello. How's it going?'

'All right so far.'

'Seen Amos and Henry?'

'Only Mr Wilks so far. I'm ... nervous about Mr Brearley.'

'Rubbish,' Matt said. He came close to her, put his arms round her, and drew her close. 'You smell of household soap,' he said.

'I've been scrubbing the kitchen floor.'

'Mm . . .' He turned her and tipped up her face.

When Amos walked in, they were kissing.

'Oh!' Amos said. He was shocked. 'I beg pardon.'

He was about to retreat. But Matt caught him and pushed him into the saloon, where Henry was pottering about setting out ashtrays. 'Henry!' Matt said. 'Can I have your attention a minute?'

'Eh? What's to do?'

'Henry – Amos – I've asked Dolly to marry me.'

Amos gave a gasp. Henry said, 'Congratulations! It's what I'd hoped for!'

'Matt,' Dolly protested. 'I thought we were going to keep it to ourselves a bit?'

'I couldn't,' he admitted. 'While I was working with Joe, it sort of slipped out. And he said Grandad said it was about time, and they were all expecting it, so I went back indoors and told Ma.'

'Oh,' murmured Dolly, remembering that Matt's first wife had been Annie's daughter. 'How did she take it?'

'Pleased as punch. She's baked us a cake.' He laughed. 'She knew the minute we turned up.'

'Er . . . when's the happy day?' Amos inquired.

'Haven't thought about that yet. We'll let you know in good time for an entry in the *Courier*, Amos.'

'Hm . . . well . . . thank you, I'm sure.'

'Let's have a drop, then, to celebrate –'

'Mr Wilks, it's not opening hours yet –'

'This is a family celebration, Amos! Nowt to do with opening hours.'

'Oh well, er . . . yes, I s'pose so.'

Henry picked a bottle of sparkling Asti Spumante from the shelf and opened it. He poured into glasses that weren't exactly appropriate, but that didn't seem to matter.

'Your health,' he said, raising his. 'Good wishes, and all that.'

Automatically Amos nodded and raised his glass.

But a great doubt was dawning in his mind. He had made

sure Matt would find out where Dolly was, with a view to having Matt bring her back to Beckindale.

But, if Dolly was going to wed Matt, would she give up her job at the Woolpack?

Fancy Matt acting so fast ... You'd hardly credit it. He'd thought it would take ages and ages before things were back to anything like normal. But, t'way things had gone, Dolly might be Mrs Skilbeck in a week or two.

'Drink up,' urged Henry. 'Drink to the happy pair, Amos.'

Amos roused himself. Well, it might all work out all right. And you had to admit they looked well on it.

He raised his glass towards them then sipped. 'Here's to you,' he said.

'Oh, Mr Brearley!' cried Dolly, delighted to be accepted back with no recriminations. 'You're so kind!'

Taken aback, Amos sipped his wine. Funny stuff – got up your nose. All the same, it wasn't bad.

Nor was it bad to see two absolutely happy people standing in the saloon bar of the Woolpack, looking ahead to a future they were going to share.

Wyndham Books are obtainable from many booksellers and newsagents. If you have any difficulty please send purchase price plus postage on the scale below to:

Wyndham Cash Sales
P.O. Box 11
Falmouth
Cornwall
OR
Star Book Service,
G.P.O. Box 29,
Douglas,
Isle of Man,
British Isles.

While every effort is made to keep prices low, it is sometimes necessary to increase prices at short notice. Wyndham Books reserve the right to show new retail prices on covers which may differ from those advertised in the text or elsewhere.

Postage and Packing Rate

UK: 22p for the first book, plus 10p per copy for each additional book ordered to a maximum charge of 82p. **BFPO and Eire:** 22p for the first book, plus 10p per copy for the next 6 books and thereafter 4p per book. **Overseas:** 30p for the first book and 10p per copy for each additional book.

These charges are subject to Post Office charge fluctuations.